StoneAge Wizard

by

Albert Samuel Tukker

You can find more information about,
and works by Albert S. Tukker at
http://AlbertSamuelTukker.com

ISBN 978-1-4116-7777-7

In Memory of
Beverly Joan
08/31/51 - 12/26/04

Twenty-years earlier...

A handwritten note in the liver-spotted hands of Miss Prillett, substitute teacher for Ms. Jane Duphon at San Pedro Junior High, L.A. Unified;

> *JT has been tardy nearly 70% of the school year. Unfortunately, it is the school's policy of 75% before expulsion. Please help me rid the school system of this slacker and keep attendance accordingly.*
>
> *Ms. Duphon*

Miss Prillett was a large, rotund woman with short, curly, grey hair and wire-rimmed glasses. The dress she had chosen for today was a black and white floral print that draped over her frame in a lumpy bulge. She looked up at the clock on the wall on her left. Another minute had passed. Four more minutes until class began. She looked out one of the classroom windows lining the wall to her right. The rain had lightened to a steady drizzle. The aroma of wet city floated in the cracked windows and filled the school. She scanned the desk for the class roster looking to find a match to the initials. Just as her eyes fixed on the roster, the classroom door opened, creaking agonizingly on it's tired hinges. She looked up to the clock, then down to the door.

The tall, lanky boy in the doorway looked frazzled. His jeans jacket was around his elbows, sweat and rain running down his cheeks. He was breathing heavily, but not gasping, his long hair matted to his red face.

"You're just in time," Miss Prillett spat, pointing out the obvious.

The boy looked up to the clock. "Yes ma'am, I am. And three minutes before the bell, too." The class giggled and murmured. The substitute sat with a blank look in her eyes.

"Your name young man," she demanded over the chatter. The classroom became silent.

"Pardon?" Justyn said as he approached his desk in the front row, the teacher two seats to his left.

"Your name," she repeated. She was beginning to get angry at the boy. His indifference was annoying.

"I'm sorry, ma'am. You just said... I...I thought you knew." He looked back at the door, then sat down at his desk. "I'm Justyn Thyme."

"That's not funny." Her anger rose, flushing her face pink. "What is your name young man?!"

"It's no joke, ma'am. I'm Justyn Thyme. Most people call me JT. You may call me, Mr. Thyme, though."

There was silence as Miss Prillett read the roster. After a moment she spoke quietly, restrained. "I apologize, Mr. Thyme. I see the humor of your entrance now. A preconceived plan?" Justyn felt her anger more than heard it.

Justyn straightened in his seat, facing the teacher for the day directly. "No apology necessary, ma'am. And no, no preconceived plan." His voice hinted at the contempt he had for her, and for most authority. "I have a problem with mornings, but I'm working at it."

"Oh?" Her anger had suddenly subsided at the thought of making an example of the boy. "And just what kind of problem, Mr. Thyme?" As the 'm' in Thyme hummed from her lips, she wished she hadn't asked the question.

"It comes too early, ma'am."

The classroom crackled with suppressed laughter. She grimaced. The boy was smooth.

And there was something else; an attraction, a magnetism, charisma. She wanted to slap him, and yet she wanted to pinch his cheek. Then the attractive girl with the green eyes and caramel skin leaned over to Justyn, laying her hand on his arm.

"What happened to you this morning, JT?" she whispered. "I waited as long as I could. What'd you do, run all the way?"

Justyn turned to her, smiled and shrugged, "My dad."

It was obvious to anyone watching that the girl with the dark skin and Mr. Thyme had a *thing* going.

And Miss Prillett was one of those watching. "That's

enough!!!" she barked, slamming her hand down on the desk. All student eyes turned forward. Her hand returned the slap with a hot, sharp pain that shot up to her elbow, but she held it there as the class shuffled in their seats and whispered.

"You there, Miss.."

The girl with the green eyes looked the substitute teacher in the eyes, "Nicci Le'Couv'ere." The French accent was inherited.

"Miss Le'Couv'ere," Miss Prillett hissed out her name as if it tasted bitter. "Down to the principle's office for talking."

Nicci's arm began its movement to swing towards the back of the room, "But I wasn't the..."

"No back talk from you young lady! I will not take that from your kind. Now get going." She leaned toward Nicci and spoke so only four other students heard, including Justyn. "Get your zebra hide down to the principals office."

As Niccole stood to leave, Justyn spoke up.

"She's right, ma'am. Several others were talking, and I.."

"SHUT UP!!!" The classroom went still. Miss Prillett then rose from her chair and leaned across the desk towards Justyn.

"You, young man, have no idea what you are doing. Or what you're in for if you associate with this..this Le'Couv'ere." She overemphasized the name, her disgust at the mixed blood blatant. "You march your little butt down to the principal's office with *her* and I'll be down after class to explain to Mr. Huttson why you're there." She paused for a moment as she and Justyn exchanged glares.

He could see her anger, her rage. He couldn't

understand why, though. What had he done? What was it to this substitute if he and Nicci liked each other?

"Go!" she commanded. Justyn stood up from his desk. "And take your things with you."

Both students gathered their backpacks and books, then left the room together. In the hallway Justyn turned to Niccole. "Let's say we skip out. Go to the park or something."

"You know we can't. We'll only get into more trouble. Besides," Niccole looked down the locker lined corridor to the end and through the glass doors outside , "it's still raining."

"Fuck the rain."

"JT!"

"Sorry. But you know all that was bullshit. Now come on, let's blow this place. You don't have dance today, do you?"

Niccole thought a moment, then agreed.

Today

It was mid-summer, early in the evening and the sun was sneaking up on the horizon with obvious intent. The few scattered clouds were turning from white to a golden hue with just a tint of red over a horizon of industrial buildings, cranes and dockyards.

Justyn Thyme stood on the small, wooden steps that led up to his home; a small, silver metal trailer sitting in the north-west corner of a boat yard in San Pedro. He closed the door then turned the key in the knob. He gave the knob a gentle tug and the door popped open. He shut the door again and headed across the boatyard to the gate in the east fence.

His tall silhouette glided across the ground with a practiced ease, moving his slender form gracefully and with purpose. The scent of wisteria and lilac mixed with the ocean breeze, filling his nostrils with nature. The scrapes and whines of cranes that echoed across and up the channel, mixed with the stench of crude oil and boat exhaust were a constant reminder of civilization. His growing hair was just to his collar. It was long enough to get in his face, but too short to tie up. He usually wore a bandanna around his head. Tonight, however, he slicked it down with gel. At nearly six feet and one hundred and seventy in weight, Justyn Thyme was a good looking man with blue-green eyes that changed hue with the light. His face had a gentle look, yet, was etched and hardened by his short time on the planet.

He had acquired the trailer in the boatyard when he became the night watchman for the place eight months ago, shortly after being hired on as yard boy. Justyn had thought it funny, Yard Boy at thirty-four. But the man who hired him, Calvin, was in his sixties, so it seemed appropriate.

Ten months ago, Justyn had decided to get himself together and off the streets. It took him two months of bus trips and hundreds of rejections before coming across Calvin and his boat yard. Calvin, boatyard owner, manager, accountant, etc., and black, had been the one to give him a chance.

Calvin's small operation was at the edge of San Pedro, the entrance to the channel a hundred yards up around the bend. Terminal Island was across the water, Neptune's Mermaids about a mile and a half further down on this side. The operation was mainly haul outs and quick repairs on site, but there was a small yard for storage and longer repairs made

7

by boat owners, and two self-serve pumps.

When Calvin discovered that Justyn was without a home, he offered him use of the trailer. The conditions were that if somebody messes with the boats, he was to call the police.

Justyn had been hesitant about taking the trailer, especially when Calvin would not take rent. "Consider it part of the salary," Calvin had said. "Besides, I'd feel better knowing someone was around after dark looking after things."

During the day Justyn would help anybody that needed it with their boat, doing what he could and learning all that he could. He had this dream of owning a boat of his own. A fixer-upper, something he could make seaworthy again.

When the opportunities arose, which was often, Justyn would have the crane operator, Marvin, show him how to lift boats out of the water and put them back in again. Marvin was also black. Marvin was also large: six foot two and two hundred eighty-five pounds but kind as kitten.

It had been their last pull of the day, a thirty-foot Cheoy Lee ketch in need of extensive hull and deck repair. As Justyn eased the ketch out of the water, Marvin said, "Went shootin' pool last night. Over at that topless place at the other end of the channel."

"Neptune's?"

"Yeah. That's it. You know the place, hunh?"

"I've been there a few times," Justyn said, his concentration on the boat rising higher above the water.

"Shot a few games with a skipper there," Marvin went on. "Captain Red Beard everybody was calling him. I got the feeling he might be in need of a crew. Nice boat. Tied up across the street. He don't talk a whole lot, but he can kick ass on a pool table. I lost every game to the hairy fucker."

Justyn had stopped the crane when Marvin mentioned crew and now stared at him, waiting for more information. When it didn't come after a moment, he prodded, "Will he be there tonight?"

Marvin shrugged. "He'd said something about heading out soon."

"He could be gone?!?"

Marvin shrugged. "Sorry, JT. Just now thought of it."

"Damn. Just damn." Justyn sat a moment looking through Marvin. He glanced back west, then back to Marvin. "Help me get this boat cradled so I can get out of here."

StoneAge Wizard

Justyn walked the two miles to the bar. The sun was approaching the horizon fast, the pink street lights coming on sequentially as shadows darkened. The street was lined with small shops closed up for the night. Justyn lit a cigarette and crossed the street. He turned right, towards the ocean, and headed downhill towards the only cross-street below.

One other person walked the street with Justyn. Coming up the other side was a woman in rags, pushing her shopping cart of belongings. In the silence between the buildings he could hear the rattling of the cart and the woman's raspy voice as she talked to herself. Moments later they passed with quick glances. Then she stopped and looked hard in his direction. Justyn had stopped too, staring back at her.

"JT?" the woman yelled.

He couldn't quite make out the silhouette across the street, but Justyn recognized her voice then. "Helen!" Justyn quickly checked for traffic, then trotted across the street.

When he reached her, Helen grabbed and hugged Justyn. Letting go, she looked him over. "You're lookin' good, JT. Real good." Her toothless grin made him smile. "Let me hit that," she said, reaching for his cigarette.

"Here." Justyn took a long drag on the cigarette. "Finish it. I need to quit anyway."

"Well then, give me your pack."

"I'm not that ready." He reached into his pocket and extracted a cigarette. "Here's a fresh one for later."

"Thank'y."

"Where've you been staying?"

"No place in particular. Can't stay in one place too long anymore. Cops start hassling ya'. Gary's on the other side of the freeway. Found him an alley behind a laundromat. Jo-Jo is still roaming up and down the beaches. Saw him the other day. He's got a dog now."

"Seen BC lately?"

"Last I talked to him was the Fourth. He's up in L.A. still. Crazy old fool is gonna get hurt up there." Helen eyed Justyn over. "Wha'cha' all dressed up for?"

Justyn glanced down at himself. He had on new jeans, a solid, button-down shirt and a faded denim jacket. He shrugged, "Heading out to shoot some pool."

"Heading for that titty bar, ain't ya'? Shame on ya'."

Helen smiled her toothless smile again, then laughed. She winked at Justyn and said, "If only I were younger."

He knew she had done some prostituting when she was younger and laughed. "If only I was more desperate."

Helen giggled. She had known Justyn for over a year now and she knew what he was looking for, "Find your escape, yet?" she asked.

"No. But I am working in a boat yard. In San Pedro. In fact," he reached into his jeans and pulled out a simple ring with three keys on it. He handed it to her. "Here. There's one for the gate to the yard. The trailer key is there, too. You can stay a few days with me if you'd like."

"You always were generous to a fault, JT. Which is probably why we all love ya'. Bless you boy. Bless you," she said taking the key. "Now. Where the hell is this place and which trailer is it?"

"It's the only trailer in the yard," he explained, then gave her the address. She whistled when he did.

"That's quite a ways for me to push this thing," she said, patting her cart. "But I'll make it just fine. You'll see." She kissed him on the cheek. "Want me to leave the gate unlocked for ya'?"

"No. I'll climb over the fence."

He gave her a hug and a twenty dollar bill.

She looked up at him and smiled. "Do love ya', JT. Really do."

He kissed her on the cheek. "Love you too, Girl."

"Now I've gone and creamed my panties."

"I'll see ya' later," Justyn said through a chuckle, then crossed back to the other side of the street and continued to the corner.

  As he neared the corner and the waterfront, the ships and work boats slowly emerged from block silhouettes. A container ship was being loaded across the channel, a row of fishing boats lining the near side. Moments later he turned left at the street corner, eyes and mind on the water, looking for a sailboat.

  Halfway down the street was *Neptune's Mermaids*. Dancing in neon on top of the sign was a figure of a woman. He returned his eyes to the water.

  He was almost at the bar before the sailboat came into view. The sun was drawing long shadows, but there was enough light to see the sailboat's lines. He crossed the street for a closer look.

  It was a schooner, two masts, the taller aft, tied stern to the dock. The hull was varnished wood from the bootstripe to the toerail, broken only by the chainplates. The trim around the windows and the sides of the cabin were also varnished, the cabin top painted an off-white with non-skid patchwork peppering the roof. The sails were tied neatly around the booms and 'stays. The deck was teak. The cockpit was just aft of amidships, which meant an aft cabin and windows in the stern. He guessed forty-five feet on deck, close to fifty overall including the bowsprit. Across the transom in script lettering, above and below the stained-glass windows, was the boat's name - StoneAge Wizard.

  "Nice", he whispered to himself, nodding. He looked at the schooner for few moments longer, then walked back across the street and entered the bar.

  Inside, Justyn handed the man behind the barred

window a five dollar bill and pushed opened the door when the buzzer sounded. Loud music and the stench of alcohol and cigarettes greeted him at the threshold. He stepped into the dimly lit room, the door clicking shut behind him. He waited for his eyes to adjust to the low light before walking into the room.

The seduced lighting on stage focused in first. The dancer caught his attention, holding it. Justyn watched as she removed herself from the pole and moved rhythmically around the stage. She knew what she was doing. Justyn felt a stir in his groin as he watched her from the side. The beat changed and she stood, wiggling her breasts as she rose. She turned his direction and danced for him. Justyn turned away from the stage and walked further into the room.

The sound of billiard balls clacking turned him to his left. There, on a raised platform sat two billiard tables, end to end, three feet apart. Justyn stepped between the break in the anchor chain that cordoned off the raised floor as another crack of billiard balls rang out. The man rising from the shot, at the left and only occupied table, wore laceless deck shoes and khaki, deck pants. Tucked into those pants was a faded blue shirt that hung loosely on his slender frame. His hair looked charcoal grey, but was actually black, streaked heavily with white, reaching below his collar in tight waves. His beard was nearly the color of his hair, except for strands of honey-red. He had let it grow until it was to the middle of his chest. Justyn would not know Jonas' name until the next day because of those honey-red strands. But it was those honey-red hairs that identified him as the skipper of the schooner.

Justyn sat down at a small table in the middle of a large

picture window. Across the street sat the schooner. That beautiful schooner that he now very much wanted to sail on.

"Nice shot, Cap'n," his opponent said after the balls settled, none dropping into a pocket. "My turn now, though." He wore a tight T-shirt that informed all about the waste of time sleep is. The large, muscle-bound opponent then bent over the pool table and attacked the balls with a wobbling cue.

Justyn looked to see that his attack on the solemn little balls had been futile and he was now coming towards him.

"Excuse me, do you know who's schooner that is out there?" Justyn asked, thumb to the window.

"That's Cap'n Red Beard's boat," the man in the T-shirt pointed with his thumb to the man playing pool. "The StoneAge Wizard. His Daddy built it in 'thirty-six. His Daddy..."

"Otis!" came the stern voice from the billiard table. It was low and dry. The large man before Justyn, Otis, turned to Captain Red Beard with the look of a puppy that had been scolded.

The man with control of the table was indeed Captain Red Beard; owner and skipper of that beautiful schooner that had immediately caught his heart. Justyn needed to talk to the Captain.

"He doesn't like me talking about him. I don't know why? I don't know shit."

"You the crew?" Justyn asked Otis.

"Nah, just keeping the Cap'n company. His old Lady's working," Otis nodded towards the stage. "You shoot?"

"Some. Names JT." Justyn stood, offering his hand. "How do I get in the game?"

"Buck-fifty a game. Challenger pays," he said. As they shuffled towards the rack end of the table, Otis retrieved his beer and continued, "He tied up two months ago. Plays most every night."

"He knows what he's doin'," Justyn said as they both watched.

"I'm lucky to get one shot a game. So I end up prodding at him for some conversation. It took me all of six days to find out about his father building the boat.

"Hell, I don't even know the dude's name. I just call him Cap'n Red Beard 'cause every one else does." Otis shrugged. "He don't seem to mind," then gulped at his beer. He wiped his upper lip with his tongue before adding, "But he sure plays one mean-fuck of a game of pool."

"Otis. Behave," Jonas said with a weariness Otis missed.

"Would you care to play winner?" Jonas asked Justyn. "Winner breaks, challenger pays."

"Sure, Captain," Justyn walked over to Jonas and shook his hand. "I'm JT. Let me catch a drink and get some change."

"You better get five bucks worth," Otis prompted as Justyn headed for the bar. Jonas continued to clear the felt.

Billiards

Justyn deftly removed the rack from the billiard balls, spun it twice between his forefingers, placed it on the floor beneath the table, then went to the wall for a cue stick. Jonas chalked his cue and waited as Justyn eyed each perspective cue for straightness. Locating one after studying several, Justyn returned to the table and the rules.

"Straight eight. No slop. No need to call, but if you mess up a shot, be honest. Integrity goes a long way here." Jonas turned to Otis, "Eh, Otis?"

Otis looked at Jonas, smirked, then sucked on his mug of beer.

"Seems fair enough," Justyn said as he turned from Otis to Jonas. "I believe it's your break."

Jonas leaned toward the lone white ball at his end of the table and fired it off the end of his stick as if it was shot out of a gun. "Sure is," he muttered just before the racked balls exploded across the table. The three and the nine ball disappeared into opposite pockets at Justyn's end.

"Still open," Justyn announced. Neither he nor Jonas spoke any louder than necessary to be heard.

Otis, though, bellowed like a moose. "Fucker breaks like that all the fuckin' time."

As Jonas lined up his first shot, he reprimanded Otis, "Keep it down. You'd think we were in a bar."

The balls were fairly evenly distributed on the felt, with a slight prejudice towards the rack end. Jonas tapped the cue ball. The intended ball fell into a side pocket. Another stripe.

"You the owner of the schooner?" Justyn offered.

"Yeah," Jonas said, the cue behind his back as he sunk another shot.

"She's beautiful."

"Yeah." Another ball disappeared into it's chosen pocket.

"He don't talk much," came Otis' baritone voice from directly behind Justyn. The volume was down, allowing some emotion out. He stepped beside Justyn and continued his biography of the Captain. "Unless it's about shooting pool or his boat out there, but even that takes some doing.

"The boat's ten years older than he is," Otis continued. "Fifty-two feet, stem to stern. The Cap'n claims it's the original hull and deck. Only the masts are new. Aluminum."

"Less weight aloft," Jonas said, missing the shot.

Justyn eyed the layout of the table as he approached it for his first shot of the game. He found a 3-ball combination.

Justyn looked up as Jonas paced down the far side of the table and saw the necklace momentarily as Jonas' beard raised with his shoulders. It was a leather bag, dark brown or black. Slightly oblong, it resembled a teardrop. Something in it formed to the bag like wet sand. It rested firmly against Jonas' bare chest.

"Original hull and deck? Since 'thirty-six?" Justyn said with a blatant air of disbelief. He turned back to the table and addressed the cue ball.

"New caulking every year or so, and I've replaced a few planks. But other than that, she's original."

Justyn lined up the shot, raised up off his stick and looked at the angle again. He shifted to his left an inch. He aimed again, inhaled, held it, then exhaled as he followed through. The shot was near perfect. Two of the three balls he intended fell into pockets. The third kissed the corner of the side pocket and bounced harmlessly away. It was Cap'n Red Beard's turn.

Justyn turned around slowly, stopping momentarily to gaze at the caramel skinned dancer on stage. Something about her was familiar. He watched her for some moments before shrugging off his attempt to remember her. He had other things on his mind and she was too far away. He continued his turn until he found Jonas studying the table from the corner pocket across from him. Otis was occupied with two dancers. Justyn smiled and shook his head. He caught the Captain's eye. Jonas shrugged.

This would be the closest he would get to winning a game against Jonas all evening.

Coffee

They had been playing pool for close to two hours. Otis, who had sucked down nearly a keg of beer and extracted Justyn's recent life history while they watched Jonas play, was now deep in conversation with one of the bouncers about the quality of American made motorcycles. Jonas had nursed his mug of orange juice and controlled the pool table the entire time. Justyn himself had had three glasses of whiskey and was feeling pretty good.

"Surely you can get a better job than a yard boy?" Jonas asked. He had just put the eight ball down a corner pocket and was unscrewing his cue stick.

Four of Justyn's balls were still on the table. He had

prodded at the Captain between Otis' questions without much result. The short answers from Jonas didn't tell him what he wanted to know: Can he crew for him? This was the first remark offered by Jonas this evening that didn't refer to the game of billiards.

"Oh, I suppose I could. But after my parent's insurance money ran out, I was on the street for eighteen of the last twenty-four months. My perspective of life changed. For the better, I'm afraid." Justyn made a quick shot at the thirteen ball.

"Besides, if I made more money, I'd have no excuse not to move. And I rather like my trailer."

Jonas put the dismantled cue in it's case, setting it in a corner while Justyn finished the table. He returned to the billiard table stroking his beard.

"You ever been sailing?" he asked Justyn.

"Love it." Justyn's mind was in a whirl. Was this it? "I used to crew on charter boats in the Caribbean. Made enough for college. Why?"

"Let's find a table and talk some." Jonas gave the pool table to Otis and stepped through the opening in the chain, grabbing his cue case along the way.

Justyn followed him to a table situated against a back wall. It was away from the other tables and relatively quiet, with a clear view of the stage. There they could converse at a near normal level.

"How drunk are you?" Jonas asked bluntly after they had sat down.

"I'm feeling pretty fuckin' good right now," Justyn boasted without slurring. "I'll be cussing my head off the rest of the night, but I can still think." Adding after a short pause, "I'm glad I walked here, though. Why?"

"After listening to you and Otis talk, I wanted to talk to you about crewing for me."

Justyn's eyes lit up like a toddlers on Christmas morn'. He straightened his posture.

"I'm heading to Amsterdam to see an old friend and lay-over for repairs on Stoney. I'll be going by way of the 'Horn."

Justyn's glow dimmed slightly at the mention of Cape Horn. "Repairs after going 'round the fuckin' Cape?"

"There's no need to worry about the 'Horn. By the time we get down there it'll be the calm season."

"I didn't know there was a fuckin' calm season for the Horn," Justyn balked.

"You've heard too many stories. Now tell me about you sailing these charters."

"It's been a few years," Justyn began. "I crewed for a company called Caribbean Sunrise Charter's. It wasn't a big outfit, but they kept all eight boats sailing most of the year. They ranged from thirty-six to fifty feet. I sailed them all, too."

"How long is a few years?"

Justyn thought for a moment, his fingers and lips moving as he counted in his head. "'Bout twelve. I wouldn't need much of a refresher course if that's what you're worried about."

"That remains to be seen. What about navigation? Any celestial, or did you use GPS?"

"The company wanted us to use GPS all the time, but after an embarrassing moment, I learned celestial."

"Care to elaborate?"

Justyn sipped at his drink, stalling almost a minute before deciding to expose himself a little. "I was crewing on a week charter. I had been with 'Sunrise for about six months then and was feeling pretty fucking cocky.

"I was at the helm explaining to this boy about GPS and it's accuracy after all the correction bullshit when he asked me what would we do if the GPS failed. All I could do was shrug. The little son-of-a-bitch started laughing at me.

"When we got back to 'Sunrise I started in on celestial navigation. I will need some brushing up on that, too." He sipped at his drink again.

"How many storms?" Jonas challenged.

"At sea?"

"Yes."

"None."

"Well then," Jonas paused, stroking his beard, "what's the worst condition's you've been in?"

Justyn sank into the chair as he plodded through the whiskey-hued haze. The music stopped and the dancers on stage changed. Justyn faintly heard the DJ introduce the next one. Moments after the song began, he recalled his worst weather conditions at sea.

He looked up to see Jonas trance-like as he watched the dancer on stage. Justyn turned his head to the right to see for himself.

The dancer moved with erotic grace. It was easy to understand Jonas' captivation. Justyn turned back to Jonas.

"Nice fuckin' tits."

"Cost her five thousand bucks." Jonas' attention was still on the dancer.

"You know her?" Justyn asked.

"You could say that. Her name's Natalie. She's coming with me," Jonas turned to Justyn, "us. She can't sail, but she can cook and sew."

"You know her pretty fuckin' well then, hunh?"

"You could say. I paid for those tits." Jonas turned back to the stage, catching Natalie's attention. She winked, then thrust a hip his direction. A wadded bill bounced off her left breast, bringing an uproar from a cluster of men directly in front of her.

When the din ebbed, Justyn volunteered his worst conditions. "Okay, the heaviest weather I was in was onboard a forty foot sloop. We had fifteen foot swells and thirty knot winds."

Jonas countered without hesitation. "Sixty foot swells, a hun'erd and ten on the wind," he gestured out the window by the pool tables. "Stoney."

Justyn let out a quick whistle. Do things really get that hairy out there? He dug out and lit a cigarette. Jonas' eyes returned to Natalie. When the song ended a few moments later, Justyn started anew.

"Everyone at the company said I was a natural sailor. A lot of the clients I crewed for spoke highly of me and requested me the next year. I almost stayed on after college."

"What prevented you?" Jonas prodded.

"I..I," he gulped his drink. "I got involved with a married woman."

Jonas gave Justyn a tired look.

"She told me they were divorced," Justyn pleaded. "Instead of alimony, she had settled for a large check. She had said he had found a younger woman.

"I found out later that she had stole the money from this prick's business account. But he was seeing a younger woman.

"Anyway, after I made him swim a half-mile to shore, Caribbean Sunrise fired me."

"What happened then?"

"I came back to the States, Dallas, and put my economics minor to use as a foreclosure officer for a bank. I made decent money, but never thought of what I was doing to people's lives." He paused, sipped, inhaled.

"I met Sally during my first year there. We married after about eight months. Things went bad right after that. We lasted another year. Been single ever since.

"I guess they had me fooled pretty fuckin' well back then. I had started a career at the bank; because of the money, not because it was what I wanted to do. I married Sally. Then divorced Sally. I had achieved the American Dream: a mortgage and alimony.

"We sold the house and I bought a condo after the divorce and stayed with the bank another nine years. Then all the shit started."

"You mean your parents death's."

Justyn cocked his head slightly to one side, "You were listening."

"Why do you think I missed those shots," Jonas said.

Justyn smiled, then rambled. "I was beginning to have my doubts and misgivings about my job and society as a whole. The reasons behind our foreclosures were more than just monetary. And the lies that all the governments tell. All the wars could have been prevented. They were all either fought for political reasons, or to pillage resources, or to try to control the world. We still look down on others to make ourselves feel bigger. We've polluted most of the water on the planet. Destroyed most of the vegetation and are making up our own. We have nuclear power and weapons. The radiation of most it will last for years. Thousands upon thousands of them. And all for power and profit. It's enough to make you want to live on an uncharted island"

"I do. Call her StoneAge Wizard."

"Yeah, well, I didn't think about sailing until it was too late. That's how bad I was brainwashed.

"I was slowly coming out of it, but mostly I felt frustration for knowing without being able to do anything about it. All I kept thinking about was quitting work, never really thinking about what I would do afterwards. This was all shortly before my father died." He leaned across the table to Jonas, "I have to admit, I wasn't a bit fuckin' sorry when he kicked the bucket. But when my mom went a few weeks later, things just went to pieces for me." He leaned back and sipped his drink. "I use to get on the Internet and read all these stories from main-stream news to alternative sources and stuff from overseas. The more I read, the more I was ashamed of who I was and what I believed in. It really shook my foundation. All I believed in had been betrayed. A lot of what I had been taught in school had been lies, half-truths and one-sided. When my parents passed as fast as they did, I just couldn't take it any longer and I snapped.

"I quit the bank and moved here when the insurance money came in. I paid off all my bills, then drank the rest up.

When the money ran out, I ended up on the streets. I had by then decided that our society was committing suicide and there was nothing I could do about it, except watch through blood-shot eyes.

"I didn't want a job. I didn't want to be any part of it any more. I didn't want to help perpetuate the madness. Laying waste to the planet we live on for baubles and gadgets. It made no sense."

"How do you propose we fix it?"

"Hell I don't know. There would have to be a lot of changing, though. For everybody."

"But this is the human race we're talking about here, JT. Can you really believe that they would give all this up? Change?"

"Don't you?"

"Not anymore."

Justyn looked hard at Cap'n Red Beard. In the dim light and loud music it was difficult to gauge the Captain's seriousness. "Is that why you stay at sea? Because you can't stand people?"

"We'll not get into that right now. We're discussing you at the moment." Jonas gulped the last of his drink and waved for the waitress.

Justyn puffed on his cigarette momentarily, then snuffed it out. "What really gets me is that it doesn't have to be this way. Man has not evolved, only his technology." He then paused and sipped his drink, realizing he had 'started'. He waited while the song ended before starting again, calming his delivery.

"Shortly after hitting the streets, I read where the CEO

of the bank I use to work for retired. He received twenty-four million dollars for his 'Golden Parachute'."

The waitress came over then, interrupting Justyn. "What'll it be, Cap'n?"

"Coffee."

Justyn pushed the half-empty glass of whiskey towards the waitress. "Me, too." The waitress took Justyn's glass and left to fill their order. Justyn lit another cigarette.

"On the streets I received quite an education," Justyn said. "I re-discovered values forgotten in the business world. My priorities went through a major overhaul. My disdain for business grew into a cynicism for nearly all of society."

Jonas nodded in understanding. "How come you want to crew?"

"While living in my mansion in the alley off Broadway..."

Jonas raised his brow, "Mansion?"

"I had two cardboard boxes."

Jonas rolled his eyes.

"I'd often go watch the boats sail up the channel, 'specially on weekends. Most were just headed for the bay, but some would go to Catalina or down the coast to Mexico."

The coffee arrived. Justyn snuffed out his cigarette and added cream to his coffee. "One morning, early, at sunrise, a little ketch came down the channel. It's lines caught my eye and my imagination took it from there. The memories of the Caribbean surfaced randomly and at will after that.

"I remembered that I didn't smoke back then, sailing those charters, and the hardest thing I drank was iced tea. I remembered the feeling of being alive. Of actually doing something. I remembered being closer to nature.

"Nine months ago I decided I had to get back to the sea. I found work and compassion in an old man with a boat yard. He gave me a job, a place to stay, and small wage so I can feed and clothe myself.

"I originally wanted a boat of my own, but with my income, I thought it might be quicker if I crewed."

Jonas studied his prospective crew with reserved optimism, ideas other than crewing beginning to grow. After only moments he sat back, warning Justyn.

"Are you ready to stop drinking and smoking? I won't have either on Stoney."

Justyn nodded. "I need to get back on the water so I can quit." He turned away from Jonas and stamped out his cigarette in the ashtray. "Both. This is my last pack in my pocket. It'll be gone tomorrow."

The song ended as Justyn chased the loose embers around the bottom of the ashtray. When the speakers fell silent, Justyn leaned towards Jonas and said, softly, "This society is killing me. I have got to get away before it succeeds. You can drop me off at any port if you don't like my work, but I have got to get away. I've got to."

Jonas looked at Justyn's eyes closely, into them deeply. After what seemed like hours to Justyn, Jonas broke eye contact.

"I'm leaving for Amsterdam in the morning. Natalie is joining me, she can cook, but she doesn't sail. I could use a crew.

"If you'd like to work for your passage plus a small salary, be dockside by sunrise. We'll be leaving shortly afterwards."

"That doesn't give me much time to get ready," Justyn thought aloud. He looked at the stage, his mind elsewhere.

"I get the feeling you won't need much."

Justyn turned back to Jonas. "No. I guess I don't. But still," he pushed his chair back away from the table and stood, "I'd better get started now." He offered his hand to Jonas. "Thanks, Cap'n. I'll see you at dawn."

Jonas had by that time risen to his feet. He took Justyn's hand and squeezed firmly. "See you at dawn then, JT."

Natalie sat on Jonas' lap moments after he sat back down. Justyn was only steps away, headed out. "That your new crew?"

"Yep." He watched Justyn leave, formulating his impression.

Natalie turned and watched, too. "Thought he might be."

Jonas looked at her with a puzzled expression, then whispered in her ear, "You're beautiful, Captain."

She smiled.

"His name's Justyn Thyme. Likes to be called JT. He reminds me some of my father."

"You know, Jonas, how excited I am about going along with you this time. Considering I don't know anything about sailing."

Jonas pulled her closer. "You know I love you, Nat."

"I sure hope you do, Old Man." She squeezed his head into her breasts. "I sure hope you do."

"Mime il poove me," he said into her mounds of silicon.

"Jonas, I have something to ask you."

He pulled himself away before the bouncers got restless, smiling. He recognized the tone in her voice. "Ask away, my love."

"Nicci wants to come along. She says she knows how to sail." It came out quick, nearly running together.

"Desiree?"

Natalie nodded.

"Why does she want to go?"

Natalie paused before telling Jonas the true reason. She really did love this old salt of a man. She wanted desperately to trust in him, believe in them. She had to tell him the truth.

"She says she knows your crew from a long time ago. Back when they where in junior high. It's a long story. Rather sad, too. She says it's the main reason she's a dancer." Natalie paused, her face poised, waiting for a wisecrack.

"Wow," was all Jonas could say. Then added after a moment, "Sure. She can go." Then, after a few more moments and a peck on the cheek, "Have her come over so we can talk."

"I'll be right back," Natalie said as she stood to leave.

*   *   *

On the walk back to his trailer, Justyn rushed the dawn, wanting to be on that schooner, sails up and pulling. He jogged from the corner to the gate and nearly leaped over the fence, excited to tell Helen the good news.

As Justyn neared his little trailer he could see that the door was open and a light on. Closer, he could see Helen lying on the couch, obviously asleep. He walked up the steps quietly, along one edge so they wouldn't moan. He thought she was going to wake when the trailer shifted as he entered.

Once inside he saw the remnants of the twenty dollars. A pizza box sat open on the coffee table in front of the couch, two pieces left - onion and pineapple. He grimaced. A large, paper cup sat next to the box. Justyn picked it up and smelled the contents. He recoiled at the aroma. Beer. It was half empty and warm. He looked around. No other cups. One empty beer bottle. He set the cup back down. "Good girl," he whispered above a breath. He passed on the pizza.

He quietly gathered his essentials and stuffed them in a duffel bag, covering Helen with a blanket during the process. Before leaving, he left her most of his pocket money, and this note:

> Helen,
>
> Found myself a boat to crew on. I'm leaving at dawn. You're welcome to stay. I left some money for you under the pizza box in the 'fridge.
> > Love,
> > JT
> PS. Tell everyone on Broadway about me. I could use the good thoughts.

Justyn put the note on the coffee table where Helen was sure to see it, then wrote another note to Calvin. In it he explained where he was going and Helen's situation. He stated he knew she couldn't perform the yard duties, but was hoping Calvin could find something for her in the office. Justyn tacked the note to Calvin's door on his way back out.

He lit a cigarette and headed back towards Neptune's,

making a mental list of things to do: His bank account wasn't much and he could get nearly all of it through the ATM. What was left could sit. He didn't like banks anymore and all that bookkeeping on a dead account made him smile. It wasn't much or dramatic, but it was his tiny revenge.

He inhaled deeply on the cigarette. That was it; write a couple notes, empty out his bank account, then set sail with a stranger to Europe.

He crossed the street at the first corner and headed for his soon to be ex-bank. He was finally getting out. What lie ahead was uncertain, but he couldn't play the game here any longer.

Welcome Aboard

"Ahoy, Cap'n," Justyn yelled as he reached the
schooner.

Jonas looked up from the bow, where he was tending
to the anchor chain, to Justyn at the stern, "Morning, JT. Come
aboard," he offered, then returned to his work on the chain.

Justyn stepped forward to the break in the lifeline,
pausing before boarding, admiring the lines of the vessel before
him. The hull was mahogany, varnished and polished so the
boat looked wrapped in glass. He looked up the masts, head
tilted back as far as it could go without toppling him over. The
main mast, the one aft, had two sets of spreaders and he noticed

the additional cable for a staysail on the forward mast.

Justyn stepped onto StoneAge Wizard's teak decks, memories and old feelings of the Caribbean returning as the boat rocked with his weight.

"Good morning, Justyn," Natalie said with genuine warmth. She was standing on the ladder in the companionway.

"Morning. And please, it's JT."

"You can call me Nat'. Come on, bring your stuff below. There's someone down here who wants to see you," she said as she ducked back down the companionway.

Justyn gave a quizzical look at the back of her head, then climbed through the doors and down the ladder after her. He stepped several paces into the saloon and stopped, facing Natalie.

"You got the V-berth," she said, pointing with her left hand. "Put your gear there. Jonas expects you to keep it clean." She then turned and sat in the settee on the port side.

Justyn tossed his one bag on the bunk, "Jonas?" Was this whom he was to meet?

"The Cap'n. His name's Jonas Castle. But you should call him Captain or Skipper," Natalie explained. Her eyes shifted down and to her left, behind Justyn.

"Hi, JT," came a feminine voice from behind him.

The voice was vaguely familiar, Justyn feeling he should know who it belonged to. He turned around.

Framed in the short passageway to the aft cabin was a pretty black woman of mixed blood. Her skin was light, like caramel. Thin, sensual lips and a button nose also indicated the racial mix. She had on a green halter top that tied in the front and setoff her green eyes; a bright green that seemed to shimmer. They held Justyn. In them he could see her apprehension, her hope. Her feet and legs were bare, cut-off blue jeans that were more like wide, fuzzy, blue bikinis wrapped her narrow hips.

He recognized her from Neptune's, the one that had caught his attention, but there was more. He recognized those eyes of hers. He knew her from before, long before. But where? When?

Time stopped for Justyn as his mind searched for those eyes through the rubble of his past. He had loved a girl with eyes like that before. A long time ago. He remembered the name at Neptune's when she was on stage - Desiree. But that wasn't her real name.

Suddenly it all came back. He remembered. It was home room, junior high. The puppy love. The hand holding. The racism. His rejection of her to please others. Suddenly he was ashamed of himself. He looked down to the deck. "Nicci, yes," he said quietly to the deck. "I remember you."

"I'm impressed. But then again, there was quite a bit of trouble I stirred up for you back then," Niccole said, stepping into the main cabin.

"I never expected to see you again," Justyn said to the deck, "Let alone that you would talk to me if I did. Not after the way they made me treat you then." Then quieter, "The way I let them do it."

"I don't blame you for what happened back then, JT. We were both young. After talking with my parents I realized that you were new to racism. I even forgave your parents. After all, they just thought they were protecting their son."

"How can you be so understanding?" Justyn

questioned, his shame obvious.

"I've lived with it all my life. Besides, I was in love with you in home room."

There was silence as she and Justyn looked at each other. He knew what she was waiting for; for him to tell her something similar. He felt his stomach knot up, and didn't know why. He had forgotten all that. Hadn't he? Forgotten all about her?

"I thought we had something back then, JT. I thought you'd be glad to see me now. I thought..." she let the thought go.

"That was a long time ago, Niccole," he said after a moment, realizing he called her Niccole, not Nicci, like he did in junior high. He saw a shadow come to her eyes. "A lot has happened to me since then. Besides," he glanced away, eyes darting from one object to another as he spoke, "I don't know what we had back then. I don't know what we could have now." He looked at her and gave her a quick smile. "I *am* happy to see you. It's been a long time."

"Yeah. I guess it was a long time ago. But us dreamers don't recognize time the way others do," a tint of hurt in her voice. "You used to be a dreamer, JT. What happened?"

"Life," Justyn said bluntly.

Niccole stared at Justyn, his flippancy something new. She didn't remember him being this way, this cold. He had asked her to go with him the night he ran away from home. When she declined, telling him it wasn't a good idea, he told her that he would stay in touch. Call her when he got settled. She waited a long time for a call that never came. She looked to the deck, wishing Nat' wasn't there.

He was right, though, it was a long time ago. Memories could have turned to dreams, dreams to fantasies. But maybe it had all been a lie, maybe it wasn't all his father's doing. "Perhaps you are a racist, Justyn," she said coldly, then quickly disappeared into the aft cabin.

Justyn turned his head and looked at Natalie. "What'd I say?"

In a tone indicating this was going to be a long cruise, Natalie said, "It's what you didn't say. You better get topsides and give Jonas a hand. We'll be leaving soon. I'm going to go make sure Nicci doesn't leave. She needs to come along."

Justyn dropped his eyes and nodded, then climbed the ladder in silence. As soon as he had left, Natalie went to the aft cabin.

Day 11

It was night, late. The wee hours. The beginning of day eleven at sea. The sky was void of clouds and moon, the stars nearly blending together. Justyn was at the helm alone, watching the sky. All the stars were bright at sea, making the constellations difficult to pick out. But he found Orion, Betelgeuse twinkling red, Rigel blue bright. Below that, Sirius, shown with a white luster. He stared at the Dog Star, thinking of the trailer, Helen, and Calvin. He wished her well, hoping she and Calvin were getting along.

He had had the night watch since leaving port ten days ago. He had managed to stay away from Niccole so far, but neither Jonas or Natalie. Both of them had been on him for the way he was ignoring Niccole. But he wasn't ignoring her. Just staying out of her way. He did watch her, thought a great deal about her, then and now. A feeling, an ember, had been growing since that first day.

Justyn checked the wind on the sails by starlight. He pulled the last cigarette from his pocket and lit it, then engaged the auto helm - bungee cords rigged from the wheel to the sheets. He then made his way forward as StoneAge Wizard sliced through the rolling swells on a close reach headed just West off South. He cautiously but nimbly stepped out onto the bowsprit and in front of the forestay. He leaned back against the cable and hooked his leg around it.

The wind here was the strongest and Justyn could make believe he was flying like an albatross. He inhaled deeply from the cigarette and closed his eyes, letting his mind sort things out in the tranquillity of the wee hours, for even here, two hundred miles from land, the world is quieter as dawn nears. The bow beneath him cut the water with a whisper, splashing a near steady rhythm as StoneAge Wizard pushed through the swells.

He didn't miss the booze, not like he thought he would. Luckily he wasn't deep into it like he was three years ago or he'd be going through withdrawal now. He will miss the cigarettes, though. He had been smoking a long time. He looked at the one between his fingers in the dim glow of dawn. It was half gone. "Couple more drags then no more suicide tubes," he said to the cigarette. "No more paying some fuckin' corporation to slowly kill me."

As the loom of the morning sun started to grow on his

left, Justyn remembered who relieved him in an hour - Niccole. Actually, it would be Jonas. They would all rise about the same time. Jonas was teaching Natalie how to sail and giving Niccole a refresher course between meals. He could tell when Natalie was at the helm too, even below decks; the boat would lurch more. Niccole though, seemed a natural sailor.

His mind suddenly took him back twenty years ago. He let the memories come to the surface. The wind helped ease the remembering and the guilt associated with it.

Justyn remembered the good times just being together. His hormones were beginning to kick in then and he was awkward and unsure of himself, but she had made him feel good, comfortable, just by being there. They would sit together at lunch. They would talk in the hall between classes. He would walk her home from school. That is, until society stepped in. He was naive and hadn't realized the implications that the difference in their skin color would cause. He remembered the look in her eyes when he told her, at his father's insistence, demand, order, that he could not see her anymore. He had seen a similar look somewhere since but once.

He thought several moments trying to remember where he had seen the look, then he knocked off the ember of his cigarette. As it hit the water, he remembered. He remembered why it was difficult to recall, too. It had been in the mirror after his mother had died. He stuffed the cigarette butt into his jacket pocket and put his head against the forestay behind him.

The wind was steady. It stayed in his hair and on his exposed skin. The air was cool and he hiked up the collar of his jacket. He let the wind take control of his soul as the memories of his mother and Niccole weaved in and out of consciousness.

The wind allowed him to sift through the memories while ignoring their pain, floating above the emotion with the twelve foot waves. It allowed him to sort through all the emotional pain bestowed on him throughout his life. It allowed him to hope.

He was thirty-four years old and didn't have anything; a house, car, career, wife, retirement - none of the American Dream. He also had reneged on dreams from his youth. As he thought back, the only decent thing he had done was quit the bank. The only time he felt alive was sailing the Caribbean. And now.

Since his days on the streets he had been trying to atone for all the pain he had given to others, real or imagined. But deep inside him he knew there was something he had to do with his life, do for the world. The world was too full of beauty and wonder to waste on corporate enrichment. There was too much wrong with society to sit idly by and let it continue. He had rid himself of feeling a part of the problem some weeks after quitting the bank. But he had done nothing since to help alleviate any of the problems of the world. He had not yet become part of the solution.

He had been wandering around too long, starting this, beginning that, never finishing either. And now he is sailing away. Away from the culture he had come to loath. He felt relief, and guilt. For shouldn't he, because he can see what's wrong, try his best to right it? Isn't that the moral thing to do? But, what can he do?

If there was such a thing as fate, it had led him here to this boat. Allowed him access to the sea again, to sort himself out. He dearly needed this.

Nearly half an hour had passed before he looked up. It was time to take a sighting, before the morning sun washed the stars out of the sky. Soon he would turn the boat over to Jonas, and Nicci. Eat one of Natalie's breakfasts, then turn in - another day at sea.

Justyn returned to the cockpit and opened a seat on the port side and removed the sextant. He moved to the starboard side of the boat and looked to the southern horizon, now well defined. He only had minutes before the stars were gone, and neither he nor Jonas wouldn't be satisfied with just a sighting of Venus. He aimed the instrument at the sky.

Minutes later, after jotting down the angles, he returned the sextant to its case and its place under the port seat. He would reduce the sights and plot them after being relieved.

With the navigation done for the moment, Justyn released the autohelm and grabbed the wheel. He adjusted the sheets and halyards, checking the fill of the sails against the reading off the compass. This is what he liked best about sailing - steering the boat. His mind returned to the sifting and sorting of memories as the rest of him attended to the outside world. He pondered the racist remark from Niccole ten days earlier. He had never considered himself one.

'What would society say?' came a voice from the back of his mind. He was surprised as an apprehension grew from the thought. No, he wasn't a racist. But he did realize that society has suppressed his desires. His mind returned again to the last fight with his father. It had been a week into the month long grounding for skipping school. For skipping 'with that nasty half-breed'.

". . .I don't want you seeing her anymore!" his father screamed at him. His father wasn't a large man and at fourteen Justyn was just as tall, only lighter. His father's voice, however, made up for his lack of size. Especially when it was empowered by rage.

Again, Justyn demanded, "Give me a reason other than her skin color, Father." His words drooled with contempt.

"That's reason enough."

"I don't understand. She's pretty. Smart. She can play the piano. ."

"Shut up about that black bitch right now or by God I'll kick the living shit outta' ya'!" His father's face flushed red, his eyes glaring.

Justyn didn't understand his father's rage. How could love, regardless of whom with, be wrong. "I think I love 'er, Dad."

It was then that Justyn's father hit hiim with a closed fist for the first and only time. Justyn took the punch standing, stepping backwards several times. He shook his head, blood seeping from his clenched lips. He looked at his father, who somehow had become less for his bigotry. Less for striking him. Less for not knocking him down. It was then that Justyn lost respect for his father.

In the pit of his stomach, just below his navel, Justyn felt a sharp pang that, as the evening wore on, subsided into a dull ache. Then a rage began to grow.

He ran away from home in the wee hours the next morning before the rage could grow into something he couldn't control. He had seen what it made his father into and being his son, he figured it would have the same affect on him - if he let it.

It was now, however, that Justyn realized that he had also lost respect for society in general back then, too, not just for his father. It was then that he had started to become a cynic. It was then that he started hating the world. It was also back then that he knew he would be suppressing the rage inside him from then on. No wonder his marriage with Sally didn't work. For that matter, any of his relationships. Forced to give up Niccole, he had loved her ever since.

He shook his head in shock at this realization. Then a voice whispered of the dreams. Dreams of loving a dark skinned woman without a face and a voice without substance.

He decided to look at Niccole with an open mind. Then he could decide if he wanted to open his heart again. 'As if you have a choice', came the voice from the back of his mind.

He did though, have another reason for not wanting to get involved with anyone - lack of belief in himself. He wasn't sure when he had lost his self-confidence. Perhaps when his parents died? No. Although his mother and he stayed in touch with letters and the occasional telephone call, the loss he felt when she died was of love gone from the Earth. He thought briefly that he had lost it after Sally left, but quickly realized she was never that important to him.

As he steered StoneAge Wizard through the birth of another day, he realized he lost his belief in himself after his tenure at the bank. It was then that he discovered that most of his beliefs, what he held important, were based on what society dictated; starting with whom he could love.

It was called 'playing the game' and he learned quickly after running away from home that being born Caucasian gave him a big advantage in playing the game. And he used that advantage. But for the wrong reasons. For the wrong dream. He ended up married to a woman he didn't love, in a job he couldn't stand, and living a life that never felt right. Justyn could see now that he had been living the dreams of others, except when he was earning tuition sailing the Caribbean. But everything else felt like nonsense. Everything felt artificial, unreal. Like life was just below the surface.

But sailing was something Justyn knew he loved. Watching the boats on the weekends when he was roaming the streets had re-ignited that love. Sailing was a part of him. He had hoped it would boost his self-esteem, but seeing Niccole again, bringing back those shameful memories, struck a blow to that idea.

But maybe that would change. He let his mind wander as the sun sneaked above the horizon, fantasizing about what could be. A short time later noises started coming from below.

Niccole

The sun was four fingers above the horizon when Justyn heard the rustling from below. Suddenly he was excited, and nervous, about seeing Nicci. The companionway hatch slid open and he felt his heart speed up. Jonas' hairy face popped through the opening.

"Coffee?"

"Yeah," Justyn replied, trying to hide the disappointment in his tone. Jonas disappeared back through the opening, leaving the hatch open.

A few moments later the doors to the companionway swung open. Niccole climbed up the ladder, glanced quickly at

Justyn, then went forward. He felt a nibble at his heart, a twinge, as he watched her make her way to the bow. The cutoff bottoms and halter top didn't help matters. Suddenly he felt he was losing her just as he was about to find her. From the depths of his heart a voice screamed in a quiet whisper - "Don't let her go!"

Justyn stood at the helm, watching the wind, the waves, and Niccole as she stood at the bow, her back to him, steadying herself with the inner stay. He watched as the wind took her hair and flailed it to one side. She had worn it long back then, too. Other tidbits of information surfaced randomly as he studied her form against the dawn sky. He remembered her family had moved from Canada just after school started that year. He remembered that she was part French and Oriental, as well as part Black. He thought it was father Black, mother French/Korean, but he didn't remember for sure, and it didn't really matter. What mattered was that her parents loved each other, and their children. And, he was beginning to believe, he could be falling in love with one of their children, again.

Jonas climbed above decks with a cup and handed it to Justyn. "I made it this morning," Jonas emphasized I, pointing to himself. "I don't know if I can handle anymore of Nat's coffee. She can cook better than my mom, but she makes lousy coffee. I think she uses seawater." He smiled, then went back below decks. He returned a moment later with a cup of his own.

"How was the night?" Jonas asked as he sat near the wheel and Justyn.

"Nice. I smoked my last cigarette and did some

thinking." Justyn paused, then added, "A lot of thinking." He raised the cup to his mouth. "Hey, this is pretty good. You gonna make the coffee from now on?"

"Nope, I'm going to show you how. I like the smell of coffee brewing when I wake up."

"Oh wonderful," Justyn teased, "another duty to perform for the Cap'n."

After several minutes of silently looking at the sea, Jonas turned back to Justyn. He watched for a short time as Justyn continued to keep most of his attention on Niccole, only giving the sea and the boat the minimum required. He followed as Justyn's eyes darted from the sails to Niccole; from the weather side to Niccole; from the masthead to Niccole.

"Justyn!" he snapped sternly. Justyn flinched at the suddenness of it. "Keep more attention to sailing Stoney. There'll be time to talk with her after breakfast."

"I don't know if I'll be able to," Justyn slipped.

"Just be yourself. If you can't be yourself around her, you've no business trying to get involved with her," Jonas said with a flair of fatherly bass.

Justyn turned his attention to Niccole again. "You may have something there, Cap'n," he said his eyes on the back of Niccole.

Jonas nodded. Then asked, "How's our heading?"

"I took some sights before dawn that I need to figure, but we're still on course by compass."

Jonas reached up and put a hand on the wheel. "Plot those sights, then eat."

"Aye-aye, Cap'n."

As Justyn climbed down the ladder, he smelled

Natalie's cooking.

"Morning, Natalie. What's for breakfast?"

"Morning, JT. Same as yesterday. Chicken and hash browns. Last of the chicken, too."

"Smells delicious. Same as yesterday," he said as he sat down at the navigation table. "I'll be over to get some as soon as I plot these." He held up his little notebook.

"It'll be waiting." Natalie fixed a plate for him and set it in a depression on the dining table, then returned to the galley and started cleaning up.

Justyn finished the navigation quickly by using the calculator, though its use was frowned upon. The Cap'n wanted sharp minds, but he was in a hurry this morning. He put the calculator back in his berth before going to the table and eating his breakfast.

When he was nearly finished eating, Natalie sat across from him and nursed a cup of coffee.

"Hmph?" he mumbled through a mouthful of hash browns.

"Waiting for the dish."

He swallowed. "Oh."

"You talk to Niccole this morning?" she asked.

"Uh, no. She didn't give me a chance." Justyn put the last bite of hash browns in his mouth.

"You going back on deck later," she suggested.

He swallowed, then washed it down with coffee. "I might," he said, pushing himself back from the table and the now empty plate. "I wish I had a cigarette."

"You out?"

"Yeah. Just this morning. Should have saved it for after

breakfast."

"Well, look at it this way, now after your next meal it won't be as bad." She put her cup down, rose, then took his plate into the galley. "You're not going to be an asshole for weeks now, are you?" she added.

Justyn was taken aback by her boldness. He almost snapped at her, but bit his tongue. He closed his eyes and inhaled deeply, expanding his chest to the fullest. He would not lose control.

"More coffee?" she asked.

"Yes, please," he said, the urge for verbal revenge gone.

She returned to the table with the pot.

"She's in love with you, you know," she said after topping off both cups and sitting down. "She has been since she was in school with you."

"Really," Justyn said.

"Really," Natalie retorted. "She doesn't realize it, though. But from living with her the last two years, listening to her go on about you, I've come to believe that she has.

"You should have seen the look in her eyes when she told me about seeing you with Jonas."

"I'm sorry," he said. "I didn't mean to sound skeptical." He could see Niccole's eyes the first day. The anticipation. The hurt. "I'm beginning to think I always have to." He picked up his cup and, just before sipping it, he whispered, "But I was too fucking stupid to know it."

Natalie didn't hear his whisper. She didn't even realize he had said anything extra at all. "Isn't that convenient. Out here in the middle of the ocean and you think you've always had the hots for Nicci.

"I'd feel the same way if we were back in the States, or anywhere else, for that matter."

Natalie studied Justyn for a moment, trying to discern his sincerity. "I've known her for two years now. The entire time we've been flaunting our tits at that shithole Neptune's.

"When you left that summer without saying good-bye, she went ahead with her plans of learning ballet. But during her second year of college, which she was supplementing by dancing topless, her father was in a car accident that nearly killed him. She quit school and dancing and stayed home to help her mother care for him until he died three years later. That's when she went back to dancing. Kinda traveled the country, going from city to city, nightclub to nightclub. Guess she was searching for something." She looked into Justyn's eyes. "You, maybe?

"Her mother died three years ago. A blood clot in the brain. That's when she came back here. She worked inland for the first year or so, then came here after her parents house sold." She sipped at her coffee, putting memories into proper order.

"Do you know she was an accountant?" She put her cup down and leaned toward Justyn. "Last year she started putting money away for dance school. Says she's wanted to dance since grade school."

"Yes. A ballerina," Justyn said into his cup.

"Well, I'll be damned. I'm impressed."

"We went through a lot."

"I know. She told me."

Justyn placed his cup on the table and looked into

Natalie's eyes. "Did she tell you about her boyfriends?"

Natalie only peered over the her cup at him.

Justyn sighed. "Was she ever married?"

Natalie put the cup down, then shook her head. "No. She was serious with this guy once, until he started talking marriage." She picked the cup up and just before sipping, said into the cup, "I don't think she ever got over you."

"Yeah, well, I'm starting to believe the same about me."

"But you didn't even recognized her on stage."

Justyn blinked, astonished she knew. Then it hit him; Nicci had seen him before going on and had pointed him out to her. "Well, the Cap'n is a demanding audience."

"Not that demanding. Not if you had always been in love with her. Knowing it or not, when you saw her dancing, and I don't care what you and Jonas were talking about, when you saw her dancing, your heart should have skipped a beat." She took a breath, a sip of coffee, then just looked at Justyn. After several moments of silence and staring into Justyn's lost eyes, Natalie explained her affection for Niccole.

"I was there when she auditioned for Neptune's and kinda took her under my wing. Kinda like the daughter I..." she sipped at her coffee.

Justyn did the same, waiting for her to go on, not knowing what to else say or do. He suddenly turned amidships, stating that he better get on deck.

As he started up the ladder Natalie said, "Don't hurt her again, JT."

"I have no intention," he said as he climbed. On deck he quickly told Jonas that they were still on course, then went

54

forward.

"Can I talk to you?" Justyn asked Niccole from behind. She was sitting on the cabin top facing forward, feet on the foredeck, arms behind her as braces. Her hair had been pulled back into a ponytail. She looked up at him.

"Sure. Have a seat, Mr. Thyme."

That hurt. "I'd like to apologize for my behavior the past few days." He sat to her left. "Especially day one, when I blew you off like I did. I didn't mean to hurt you. I..uh..well, I was taken by surprise."

"What makes you think you hurt me?" Niccole snipped.

Justyn let it slide, then said, "I've had some time to remember. I've even done some soul searching. The ocean does that for me."

Niccole looked at him. "Does what?"

Justyn looked out to the water ahead. "Allows me to be," he turned to her, "me."

"You mean, out here, where no one can see us, you think its okay to be with me." Her eyes were cold, her upper lip trembling.

"Wha...hunh..? Where did that come from?"

"You said your father wanted us to break up. It was really you who wanted to end us. Wasn't it?" She was near tears.

Justyn held back the urge to pull her close. He looked to the water again. "It was my father's demand. I disobeyed it. But I had to runaway before my father did something stupid." He turned to her and found her looking back, eyes screaming for him to hold her. "And you wouldn't come with me then.

55

What was I to think? I thought you didn't love me. That's why I thought you wouldn't go." He turned away, eyes to the water, seeing nothing. The sea whispered things to him he couldn't hear as he and Niccole sat quietly.

This wasn't going as he had hoped. He had envisioned her forgiving him for the last few days, and the last twenty years. Then StoneAge Wizard lurched to starboard.

The next moment found Justyn with Niccole in his lap, face up. "You all right?"

She hesitated. "Fine. Help me up."

When Niccole was sitting up on her own, Justyn asked, "Why didn't you go with me?"

"Hunh? When?"

"Junior high."

"I was afraid of what would happen to us; by people who didn't view the world as we did."

"That didn't concern me. It only bothered my father."

"Yeah? Well, it scared the daylights outta me."

"I wish I had known."

"You would've if you had called?"

What can he say. I didn't call because I was mad at you for two years? "I'm sorry. I thought it wouldn't have mattered. I thought you had stopped loving me."

"Not one minute."

He turned to find her staring at him, her eyes grabbing his instantly. As the boat pitched and rolled, he found himself falling into their depths.

He was going to hate himself, but he had to tell her. "I haven't thought about you since junior high. That's why I didn't recognize you on stage back there."

"What are you trying to say, Thyme?"

"On day one, when I first saw you in the doorway of the aft cabin, my heart jumped. Then, as I was climbing the ladder to help cast off, after seeing the hurt I caused, I felt lousy. I haven't been able to keep you outta my head since. Good thoughts, bad memories, good memories." He braced himself, then reached over and touched her hand. "I'd really like to get to know you again. I really would."

"Just like that. A fast apology, some honesty, and bam! I'm suppose to jump into your arms."

"Whoa. What the hell?"

"Sorry. Nat' and I were talking earlier and..."

Justyn put a hand up, indicating for her to stop. "'Nuf said. We had the same one, I think, just before I came up here."

"Busybody ol' bitch."

"Nicci!" Justyn exclaimed in mock shock. "In Junior high you used to chew me out for cussing."

"Oh, piss off."

They laughed. Then stared into each other's eyes for a few moments, then turned and watched the ocean flow to them.

Hearts for Dreams

They were sitting in the cockpit, Justyn steering with his feet. Niccole sat on the weather side, starboard, the wind flicking tendrils of hair into the air like little whips. This was day thirty-one and they were within a day of Cape Horn. Niccole had been on night watch with him for about ten days. As he watches her now, he wonders if he ever did stop loving her.

That could explain all of his failed relationships. His inability to find happiness, contentment, anywhere in his life. That is, until he started planning on getting a sailboat of his own. Thoughts of sailing away made him happy. Dreaming of fixing up the pocket cruiser in the southwest corner of Calvin's boatyard kept him going for weeks at a time. The little cruiser was built for coastal sailing: hundreds of miles if you wanted, as long as you kept the shore close. Justyn figured he could fix it so he could island hop across the Pacific. He always wanted to go to the Galapagos Islands to see the tortoise. And they sailed by it about eight days ago.

The setting sun lit Niccole's hair with glints of diamonds. Justyn, watching her watch the sea, noticed the glitter and wondered briefly what would cause that before realizing it was the salt in her hair. Water was a little low right then. It hadn't rained in ten days and they hadn't stopped in fifteen He turned to her and said, "This is why we didn't stop at the Galapagos, or hardly anywhere else."

"What is why?"

"The weather. We'll see the tip just after dawn."

"Oh big deal. We could have spent a day at the islands."

Justyn shrugged. "It would have been nice, but a day wouldn't have been enough."

"Yeah. A month would have been nice."

"A month!" Justyn guffawed.

"Shhh!"

"Yeah, a month would be nice."

"Maybe we can stop on the way back."

"Hunh? Stop where on the way where?"

"The Galapagos. We can stop on our way back to L.A."

They sat in silence as the boat danced through the swells. Several minutes passed, the sun setting quietly, the air cooling several degrees.

"I'm not going back to the States," Justyn announced.

"Wha..? Why not?"

He shrugged, never having thought out the statements to explain his reasoning. "Don't really like it there."

"What do you plan on doing?"

He shrugged again. "I dunno. Stay with Jonas, maybe. Hop off on some island. Maybe Europe. Maybe Africa. I dunno.

"But just thinking about going back there gives me visions of putting a gun to my head."

"JT! I'd rather hear you cuss then say shit like that."

Justyn watched the sails. He really did not want to go back to the States. When Jonas asked him on, he thought he was rid of the place. But with her aboard, and feeling the way he does about her, he had become a little apprehensive about his future. "You scare me, you know."

She looked a little stunned. "How do I scare you?"

He looked her straight in the eyes. "I would give up my dreams for you."

Breakfast at Natalie's

Thirty days later they were headed ten degrees west of north, four days from their Caribbean port. Niccole was at the helm. It was morning, the sun just now leaving the horizon off the starboard side, it's warmth heating the air and bare skin. The clouds were high, scattered and blown, brush strokes against the blue.

They had had clear skies and a brisk twenty-knot breeze that scooted them around the tip of South America in less than a day. The landscape, first down and then up the coast of the continent, had been spectacular. Niccole was impressed with it all. She was a bit disappointed they hadn't stopped at the

Galapagos Islands, but the few small ports they had pulled into were each wonderful. She just wished they could have stayed longer in each. But Jonas had some schedule he was adhering to and a week in the Caribbean was pushing it. Her relationship with Justyn was, well, she really liked sailing Stoney. Maybe she could see not going back home. But then comes the question, how to get a boat of their own?

Still, she wondered what was going to happen after the cruise. Neither she nor Natalie were returning to Neptune's. Except for being with Justyn, her future was open and uncertain, which only seemed to add to her now heightened sense of being alive.

Niccole unzipped her jacket and glanced to the sky, then back to the sails and the water ahead. Jonas and Justyn were below going over the charts, Natalie was banging and clanking in the galley preparing breakfast. She glanced down at the compass, then to the sails, studying the wind in them. She gently turned the wheel. The sails filled a little more, then spilled some as StoneAge Wizard heeled a few more degrees. She glanced back at the compass. Pretty close. She reached over and pulled in a bit on the jib sheet. She checked the sails once more, then returned her gaze to the water, her mind only part there. She was getting excited about the Atlantic crossing and seeing Europe.

Justyn had promised her earlier that morning that he would show her how to navigate using the stars while they crossed the Atlantic. Neither him nor Jonas relied much on electronics, though the radar unit was always on.

She had asked Jonas shortly after leaving Los Angeles why he ran the radar constantly. His reply:

"Going into port it shows me landfall. All the time it gives Stoney a nice big blip on those tankers radar screens. That's especially nice in that big, wide open ocean out there. Keeps them smelly things from running your ass down..."

The mainsail fluttered and she realized she wasn't paying close enough attention to the task at hand. She tore her thoughts from her reverie and back to the boat.

Jonas' father had rigged all the control lines to run to the cockpit so she didn't need to leave it, but she did need to leave the wheel. She lashed the helm with bungee cord and went about trimming the sails.

She had come to love this boat and to respect the man that had stole her best friends heart, and allowed her to find hers. Jonas came up the companionway as she unlashed the wheel.

"Better go below and get some breakfast before JT eats your share too," he jested.

"Aye-aye, Cap'n," Niccole said with a smile. She moved to one side to let Jonas in behind the wheel. When he had hold of it, she leaned backed towards him and quickly gave him a peck on the cheek.

"What was that for?"

"For letting me come along. I don't think I've ever been happier," her effervescence made her eyes sparkle. "The weather has been beautiful, the sights breathtaking, and I have JT back in my life."

"My pleasure, my dear," Jonas said, tipping his head slightly towards her. "My pleasure entirely. Although, I had nothing to do with the weather, the sights, nor JT."

Niccole stood beside Jonas for a moment, feeling the

wind on her face and through her hair. After several minutes she breathed in deeply and held it. She let it out slowly, then said to Jonas, "I could live out here."

"I do. Have all my life."

"You love it, too."

"Quite so. I'd die if I had to live on a land."

"Oh, you would not," she scoffed.

"Yes, I would, of a broken heart. Same as if I lost Nat'."

She looked at him, studying his eyes as they watched the sea. "Ya' know, I believe you would."

He nodded without turning away from the sea. Minutes more passed as she absorbed more wind, more of him. He was an extremely sensitive man. He did belong out here. And perhaps, she too. Again, she broke the silence.

"They should outlaw boats with motors."

"Hey now, Stoney has an engine."

"I mean only sailing ships should be allowed."

"Yeah. And horses instead of cars."

They turned and looked at each other. "JT feels the same way," Jonas said, then added, "Speaking of which, you better go get breakfast."

"Aye-aye, Cap'n."

Niccole pecked Jonas on the cheek again, then lighted to the companionway, disappearing through the opening effortlessly.

As she glided down the ladder, Niccole said to Natalie, "That Jonas of yours is such a special man."

"I know," Natalie replied. "That's why I love him. You ready for breakfast?"

Niccole sat across from Justyn at the table and nodded at Natalie. Justyn was finishing up his breakfast with a cup of coffee. She kicked off a shoe and caressed his lower leg with her bare foot. "Why is he so special?" he asked her.

"Because he's a decent, thoughtful, generous, loving man," Natalie said from behind. She left the galley and sat down next to Niccole, placing a plate of pancakes and powdered scrambled eggs in front of Niccole.

"I have to agree with her," Niccole said as she poured honey over the entire plate.

"I've known Jonas now for going on four years," Natalie began, cradling her coffee cup in her hands, elbows resting on the table. "The first time he was in Neptune's he shot pool by himself the whole night. I tried to strike up a conversation with him, but he didn't say a whole lot. Just smiled at me and asked my name. I couldn't get his name. I couldn't talk him into a lap dance. All I got was smiles and my drinks paid for. I started calling him Cap'n Red Beard that night. To his face." She reached over and gave Niccole's arm a squeeze, "Know what he did?"

"Smiled," Justyn interrupted.

After a lengthy stare, Natalie continued her story. "The next night he was in again. I saw him at a pool table while I was on stage. He had stopped shooting and was watching me dance. I don't know why, but I became self-conscious and started messing up, loosing the beat and missing steps. I didn't face his direction too much that dance.

"Then, just before the song ended, he came to the stage and tossed a bill up. He had twisted it into a tight wad. I gathered my things and the money as usual at the end of the dance.

"When I was back stage I straightened out the money. The one Jonas threw looked like a joint, the way he had twisted it. I untwisted it and nearly screamed. It was a hundred dollar bill!"

Justyn let out a whistle. Niccole shushed him. Natalie just kept on talking, sipping coffee at strategic pauses.

"I got out front as quick as I could and found Jonas, still at the pool table, still by himself. I asked if I could shoot a game with him and he said he'd rather talk.

"We sat at a table way in the back. We talked mostly about me. My past, what I liked, didn't like. He even asked me about my dreams and why I had taken up nude dancing."

"Why did you?" Justyn interrupted.

"JT!" Niccole exclaimed.

"It's all right. I don't mind," Natalie said. "I became a dancer after my husband left me. I was twenty when he ran off with another guy! I couldn't believe it - my husband a fag. That messed me up for a while, I tell ya'.

"I tried some office jobs, but could never get the gist of things. Also, the pay really sucked. And usually the boss wanted me to, too.

"I was barely making it when a friend suggested I try dancing topless. I have to admit, the thought of dancing naked for a bunch of drunks scared the hell outta me, but she talked me into it; telling me the pay was real good and the bouncers guarded ya' really well. After my first dance I was hooked. What an ego boost. I forgot all about my fag ex'.

"That was back in San Diego. A long time ago. I moved around a lot before ending up at Neptune's. It was going to be my last stop. I've been saving and was getting close to retiring when Jonas entered my life. And now that I'm with Jonas, I guess Neptune's *was* my last stop." She beamed a smile at Justyn that showed the etched lines of a hard life.

He wondered why he hadn't noticed before. She was still attractive, just not as young as he first thought. She had around ten years on Justyn.

Natalie's long, auburn hair that brushed her shoulder blades was void of grey. Shorter than Niccole, she was slightly heavier. She was adorned with freckles. Her mouth was wide and sensual, her nose broad and short. Her eyes were warm and sorrowful, and a smile "...that touches your soul", as Jonas had said.

"Jonas didn't ask to take me home that night," Natalie went on. "I didn't understand. He tosses me a hundred dollar bill so we can talk half the night, but he didn't want to take me home." She turned her eyes to Niccole, "You know how they all think we're whores."

Justyn lightly coughed. Natalie gave Justyn a sideways glance that made him crave an unfiltered cigarette.

"I asked him why he gave me the hundred bucks, and he says he wanted to get my attention.

"I didn't know what it was about him, but when he just waved and said, 'See you soon' as he was walking out, I was hurt." With that, Natalie stood and slipped into the galley.

"Anybody else for more coffee?" she asked, returning with the pot.

"I'll take a cup," Niccole said.

"Me too."

Natalie poured everyone a cup, then placed the pot

back in the galley before sitting back down. "I watched for him all that next evening, hoping he would come back," she started after sipping at her cup. "I wanted to blow him off and try to forget about him, but I kept catching myself looking around for him. Then, halfway through my shift, after a lap dance, I saw him shooting pool by himself again. I went over to him as soon as I could and we talked again for the rest of the night. Cost him another hundred bucks, too.

"A week later we went sailing." She raised the cup and sipped from it several times before continuing. "I was loving it at first, but when we got past the breakwater and out into the ocean swells I got seasick and we had to turn back. I felt so bad about getting sick it made the seasickness even worse. I was dry heaving until we got back to port and were on dry land. I was so embarrassed." Natalie sipped at her coffee, eyes in the cup as she remembered.

"He stayed in port for almost two weeks, coming in to shoot pool and talk to me each night I worked. We went sailing once more before he left. I'm still not sure how he talked me into going again, but I'm sure glad he did. We had a wonderful time, specially since I didn't get seasick."

"How long were you out sailing?" Niccole asked.

"Just a couple of days. We went to Catalina, but that wasn't our plan. We had left before noon and was going to stay out to watch the sunset from the water. He tried to show me how to steer the boat while we sailed around waiting for it, but we ended up just sitting and drifting and talking.

"Finally the sun went down. It was my first sunset on the water. Oh, was it beautiful! The most beautiful sunset I'll ever see. I'll never forget it. And the night sky afterwards. The stars!"

"What about Catalina?" Niccole prodded.

"During the sunset Jonas asked me if I wanted to sail to Catalina for a day with him.

"I was hesitant, but something told me it would all be fine. Hell, I was attracted to the old salt. Infatuated." She shrugged, then leaned closer to Niccole and said, "Hell, I was already falling in love with him, and I think he picked up on that.

"The wind picked up after the sun went down and we sailed through the night to Catalina, arriving before dawn. We anchored in a small cove on the far side and ate breakfast in the cockpit after Jonas 'battened down the hatches'." Again she leaned close to Niccole before adding, "He cooked me up a wonderful breakfast," then, as she straightened back up, "So don't let the old salt fool ya'. He can cook if he wants to."

Justyn smiled into his coffee cup.

"Anyway, we sat there after breakfast and watched the birds fish as he told me of his life." She paused and turned around, looking out the cockpit at Jonas. His eyes were out to sea. He was sailing. He wouldn't miss her. Natalie turned back to the young lovers.

"He told me of his father's hatred of the oil companies. Said his father didn't like the pollution it caused. Or the wars fought over it. He said his father didn't like the way they were making all that money at the expense of the planet when it was so unnecessary and harmful. His father had been an accountant for one of them. I can't remember the name of the company, but they've long since been gobbled up by one of the bigger ones.

"His parents lived on the east coast and his father didn't like the way civilization was turning out. So, he embezzled a bunch of money and ran away with his wife to South America. There he invested the money and built Stoney. Ten years later, on board this boat," she leaned towards the keel and looked forward, "up there in the V-berth, Jonas was born."

"Wow," Niccole breathed.

"How much money did his father steal?" Justyn asked.

Niccole looked at him with stern eyes.

"I don't know," Natalie shrugged. "Enough for Jonas to never have to work a day in his life. His father also invested wisely. That's all he told me.

"I do know that Jonas has never worked a day since I've known him. He'll make a business call now and then, but that's about it. He hasn't stayed in any one place for very long, either. I think the longest was two years on some island over near Fiji. I guess his father's dislike for the world had rubbed off on him." She sipped at her coffee.

"When Jonas was sixteen his father was lost in a storm. His mother died two years later. Jonas says of a broken heart." She leaned towards them, glancing back to make sure Jonas wasn't approaching. Then, in a loud whisper, "He had her cremated. He keeps some of her ashes in a leather pouch around his neck. I think it's gross, but it's his mom."

Justyn remembered the bag he glimpsed hanging from Jonas' neck back at Neptune's.

"He's been sailing StoneAge Wizard alone ever since." Natalie leaned back. "On the way back from Catalina I told him that I was falling in love with him and wanted to go with him wherever he went.

70

"That was four years ago. Now, I'm finally going."
Natalie shrugged, then stood. "I better get on deck."

The Environmentalist

Ten days later StoneAge Wizard laid at anchor in a secluded cove of Antigua Island in the Caribbean. It was late afternoon, the unhindered suns rays cut through the clear water at a narrow angle, striking the fish on their sides. They had been in Antigua a week today and were leaving for Cape Verde in the morning. Earlier that morning Jonas and Natalie had taken the dinghy ashore, leaving Niccole and Justyn stranded aboard StoneAge Wizard. "Errands," was all Jonas had said.

Justyn and Niccole sat on the stern of the boat, legs dangling over the transom, feeding old bread to the fish. Justyn broke off some more bits from the hunk of loaf he held and scattered them to the fish. Niccole watched a small piece sink in a slow, swaying motion till a small silver and blue fish snatched it from sight, leaving only a trail of bubbles. Niccole touched Justyn's hand, drawing his attention away from the grain feeding frenzy to her.

"Feel like shore food tonight?" she asked.

"Hadn't really thought about it."

"I'll buy," she offered.

Justyn smiled at her. "I'll buy. Jonas gave me a raise."

"No, you need to save your money. Build up a savings, a cash base."

"I don't need money."

"Oh yes you do. You gotta buy me a boat."

Justyn met Niccole's stare.

"What are you going to do, JT?"

Justyn turned to the water. "I don't know. I haven't given it much thought." He looked at the water a little longer before finding her eyes again. "I had no intentions of going back. I was planning on hanging with Jonas as long as he'd let me. I didn't expect to run into you."

"What if the Cap'n didn't want you hanging around after this trip? What were you going to do then?" She paused, then with more concern, "What are we going to do now, JT? I want to stay with you and if that means staying out here," she looked up to the coast, "I can take that."

"There is a pocket cruiser back at Calvin's." Justyn brought his legs up and crossed them underneath him. He broke another hunk off the loaf and preceded to break it up into little pieces. "Wonder how much ol' Red Beard likes me?" He looked back to the water and tossed out a handful of crumbs.

"I don't think that much. I made about nine hundred a week dancing, you know."

Justyn's mind started calculating, back from his banking days. If they put only half of that per week into that boat at Calvin's, he could have it ready for sail in six months. Then reality snapped back into place. "Uh, no. I'd prefer you didn't dance anymore. Unless it's just for me, of course."

"Are you ordering me not to dance?"

He paused for effect. "Yes, I guess I am."

She glared at him, as if furious. But she couldn't hold it. "I'll let you have that one. But that'll be the only one."

He threw a handful of crumbs to the fish and scooted closer to Niccole, their hips touching. "I haven't felt this calm inside," he turned to Niccole and looked into her eyes, "this peaceful about things in.." he paused as he traversed back through time in his head. He glanced to the water and back. "In a long time. I know a lot of it is because of you, but back that night Jonas and I first met, I felt a relief when he agreed to take me on as crew. Like there was chance for me to have a life after all. Not some dreary nine-to-five mundane routine that drives people insane. Nope. Society's not taking this kid."

"What's that suppose to mean?"

"Cigarettes and liquor. I could never find a good enough reason to stop my overindulgence in either of them. Life seemed easier with 'em. I've since realized they were only making it shorter.

"But, that was okay back then. If my life was some repetitive, work my ass off to help someone get richer, I didn't mind it ending a few years shorter.

"That's why I can't go back. Out here I'm away from

society and its stress. I can relax and enjoy life out here. Feel life.

"I don't have to witness the madness of business first hand or endure the stupidity of the masses and the lies of the politicians out here. I don't have to be constantly reminded of the way we treat our home, this planet." Justyn looked back to the water before continuing. "Reminded that I can't do anything about it, either. Back there, I'd light up and drink up, hoping it would make life shorter. Putting a smoky glaze over my view in the mean time."

Niccole tossed a handful of bread crumbs into the water. She watched as the fish attacked it with voraciousness. After several moments she asked, "What makes you think you have to do something about it?"

Justyn shrugged. "Somebody has to. And it's more than just setting aside a few acres here and there and burning cleaner oil." Justyn shook his head, "Cleaner oil. Who are they trying to fool?

"It requires a change of lifestyle, globally."

"Change of lifestyle? To what?"

"I'm not sure. Agrarian. Caretakers."

"What??"

"What else could be our purpose in life? Certainly it's not to exploit and pollute the very planet we live on for the sake of gadgets and monetary profit?"

"JT!? When did you get to be an environmentalist? And such a cynical one."

He shrugged again. "I dunno. I guess I've been growing an awareness since leaving the bank. No. Before." Justyn tossed another handful of bread crumbs to the fish.

"I just feel like I should be doing more for the planet than just recycling my newspapers and cans. I mean, the job I had at the bank as a loan officer, now, looks like nothing more than something to keep people busy.

"Maybe that's where we get the word business: To keep people busy, so they won't notice the madness.

"But all it did was cause stress and waste. Stress on me and the customers, and mountains of paperwork, in triplicate. And for what? Money. Profit. Always more profit. I can still hear my boss," Justyn changed his voice, Niccole assumed to imitate his former boss, "'Business has no morals. Now do it!'

Justyn returned his voice to normal. "He was always screaming at me it seems. The man had an ugly voice. Raising the volume only made it uglier."

"I remember junior high, JT. I remember how you were." Niccole put a hand on Justyn's arm. "You weren't cynical. You weren't mad at the world. Sure, you were rebellious, but what teenager isn't? You were filled with life. Happy. Always doing something fun."

"Yeah, I got into a lot of trouble that way, too."

"Oh, JT. You could find joy just by watching the clouds. I remember, I watched them with you."

The concern in her voice put a lump in Justyn's throat. What had happened to him? What had happened to the enjoyment of living? Had it been consumed by consumerism? Until he started work with Calvin he had dreaded the days, and the hope for something better come the morning had long faded. He had stopped living and was only existing. Except for the dream of sailing that kept him from lying down and waiting to die, life held no interest for him. It was that hope that put him at Calvin's boatyard, and that same hope that sent him to Neptune's Mermaids that night nearly three months ago.

"Believe me, Nicci, I use to be a lot worse than this. It's only been since the streets that I've started to enjoy life more. Even more since setting sail with you. Jonas and Natalie are assets, too."

"What's this I hear? Bank talk?!" Niccole teased.

Justyn shrugged. "Eh, you get my drift."

"Yeah, I get your drift. What I don't get is how come you're so down on life? What made you so cynical? What happened to you, JT?"

Justyn stood straight up, uncrossing his ankles once standing. He took off the tattered T-shirt and, without a word, dove into the water amongst the fish, scattering them in a blink.

Niccole watched Justyn glide beneath the surface, leaving an arc of bubbles. He surfaced some yards out, shaking his head. His growing hair splayed out in a fan about him, tossing out water droplets in concentric rings. She thought how he looked more like a seventeen year-old boy instead of a middle aged man.

"Join me till they get back," Justyn yelled to her.

She stood and removed her shirt, then dove into the water.

A Tender Ride

Only the sun's loom remained as Niccole sailed
Stoney's tender ashore, the water reflecting the lighter sky. The
shoreline was dark, except for the lights from town further
down the shore. She sat in the stern, one hand on the tiller, the
other handling the sheet. Justyn sat amidships on the weather
side, his hair in a pony-tail, watching the sail.

"I wish you'd let me sail," Justyn whined. "You don't
know this cove."

"Neither do you," she snipped back. "Besides, it's my
turn. You sailed in and back last time." There was silence as
she adjusted the sheet, then the tiller. After a moment, she
leaned back against the side and put her foot on the tiller. "You
know, I've always meant to ask you something and I guess now
is as good a time as any, Thyme."

"Oh yeah? And what question would that be, Miss Le' Couv'ere?"

"Who's idea was your name?"

Justyn looked at Niccole in the fading light, then to the sea behind her. "My father thought it would be an asset. A name people would remember. I hated it for a long time, then I found I could have fun with it.

"Remember that day in Ninth grade. We had that substitute, Prichet."

"Prillett."

"Yeah, Prillett. Big ol' gal. Remember I was almost late and what she said when I walked in?"

Niccole thought a moment, the chuckled. "Yeah. She said, 'You're just in time.' And you said, 'Yes, and before the bell, too.'"

"It got the whole classroom giggling. I'm just glad no one ever found out my middle name."

Instantly Niccole asked the obvious. "What is your middle name, JT?"

"Promise not to laugh?"

"Why would I laugh?"

Justyn looked up to the sail, then the clouds, then back to Niccole. "Because it's Marx. With an x."

"Justyn Marx Thyme. I like it."

"My father used to be somebody else. I wish I could remember that man. But all I recall is the hatred that started in Junior High."

"Because of me," Niccole nearly whispered.

Justyn turned and placed his hands on her knees. "No. Not because of you. It was all him. There was no reason for it. I never did understand it."

"Thanks. That helps. A little." She checked the sails, then looked back into his eyes. "I felt so guilty when you ran away. Like I was to blame for coming between you and your father."

"No. No, hunh-uh. It had started long before you entered my life."

"Thanks, again.

"Now tell me, Thyme. What's made you so cynical?"

Justyn turned and faced the bow.

"JT!" she said sternly. "You tell me about this now, or..," she paused as she thought up a threat. He turned back and gazed into her eyes. "Or I'll stay here when Stoney departs for Amsterdam." She saw his face soften with resolve.

"You don't have to get mean," Justyn feigned being hurt. But the acting wasn't all acting. The sudden thought of losing her had an effect on him that he wouldn't have imagined. He felt his world collapsing again, as it did after his mother died. "You wouldn't really do that, would you?" He felt like a child asking her that, but it just came out.

"You're stuck with me now. 'Til the end of time, Thyme."

They sailed several minutes in the silence of the water passing by the hull and the wind through the sail. The wind was coming off the shore tonight, so Niccole had to tack every few minutes. After a port tack, which left him clear of the mast, Justyn turned his body aft.

"Remember when I told you about the time I spent on the streets?" he asked her. She nodded. "I left a part out. I met a man I help put there."

"What?"

Justyn inhaled deeply, holding it before letting it burst out in a loud sigh. "It was a chilly night and I was trying to sleep by some electrical equipment to stay warm when this guy shows up. I started to say something when I recognized him from somewhere, but couldn't remember where.

"He recognized me, too. But he could remember from where. When he introduced himself, it all came back. He had had this company that the power company wanted put out of business. Only he was doing real good business."

"Did this guy have a name?" Niccole interrupted. "Or are you going to keep calling him This Guy?"

"His name is Brian Christianson. Everyone on the street just called him BC. Okay?" Justyn paused, waiting for a response. She nodded for him to continue.

"He was installing solar panels and solar water heaters in houses all over Texas and New Mexico, and was expanding into Arizona. He gave his customers pamphlets on how to conserve electricity and live using solar power. The electric company ended up buying back power from a lot of BC's customers. They tried to buy BC out so they could shut his company down, but he wouldn't sell. He told me it was about more than just money. BC said it was about giving the planet back to the people, ending the use of fossil fuels and nuclear energy, and giving the planet a chance to heal.

"When he wouldn't sell, they harassed and followed him everywhere. Hounding him on selling out. Then things started to happen. Shipments arrived late, or not at all. Calls to the supplier assured him that the goods were on the way. Business began to suffer because BC couldn't install what he didn't have.

"That's when they enlisted me." He turned his gaze to the center of the tender. "For a five thousand dollar bonus, I lost some documents and rushed the foreclosure on his business loan." He looked back into Niccole's eyes. "We even took his house."

"JT. How could you?" The disappointment in her voice nearly broke his heart. He so needed her approval, her love.

He dropped his eyes again. "I thought the money would save my marriage. All it ended up doing was going to Sally after the divorce." He shrugged. "I've hadn't had much need for money since then."

"You were married?!?"

Justyn nodded.

"Did you love her?"

Justyn looked out to sea.

"How long?"

"Little over a year."

"How much is a little?"

"Two weeks." He turned back to Niccole, searching her eyes, trying to find a spark. He didn't believe she didn't want to love him anymore; not after what Natalie had told him, what Jonas had told him; not after waiting twenty years. "Divorced nine."

"Weeks?"

"Years.

"I told you I've been a fool," he said and looked back to the water. After a moment he looked into her eyes again.

"All my attempts at love after junior high failed because of you. I know this, now."

"Do you know how to love, JT? Do you know what love is?"

Justyn sat quiet for a moment. Then with uncertainty he said, "Sure."

"How!? You just said all your attempts had failed. So how can you know?"

"Because my attempts failed. Because of my marriage that didn't work. That's how I know. I know how it doesn't feel. And I haven't felt the way I do now since junior high." He looked away from her and back to the water.

"I didn't know why my life was so screwed up." He looked back at Niccole. "I.."

She had grabbed hold of his eyes with hers. She was searching their blue-green color. Searching him. She did still want to be with him.

He let her in, into his soul, searching it with her. Time ceased to exist while their eyes swam in the depths of the other's. The motion of the boat became a part of them, they a part of it.

Justyn wanted to grab her, pull her into him, scream at the top of his lungs that, yes, he did indeed love her, would give his life for her, and too, that he needed her to love him. Instead, as he held her with his eyes, he said, "I really do love you, Nicci'."

Niccole kept hold of his eyes for a little longer. "You think so."

They sailed a few moments in silence. Justyn listened to the lapping of the water at the bow, the wind adding white noise to the memories on the street. He was wondering how Helen was when Niccole's soft, rough voice broke in.

"I still don't get how meeting BC made you a raving cynic."

"I'm not a cynic. And he just pointed some things out to me. Now, I..I just don't agree with the way things are. I'm frustrated I can't do anything about it. That's why I want away from it all." He looked into her eyes again when he heard her giggle. In her eyes he could see she was only searching for an understanding. Her own understanding of him. He tried his best to explain. "That's why I'm here. My contact with civilization is minimal out here."

"I'm here because of you."

Justyn looked to the bow. God he felt wonderful. Away from society, on the water with the woman he loves, has always loved, life was just getting better everyday. He was seventeen again, but not as naive.

"Besides, BC was the cynic. He hated almost everything about society, from the government to designer labels. He was trying to change things, for the better, he thought. What the bank and I did to him broke him financially."

"How come he talked to you at all?"

Justyn sighed. "We didn't break his spirit. He wanted to find out why I was there and if there was anything he could do to help. Even though he was destitute he was still fighting society in his way. I guess he also thought he was still being watched then. He thought I was one of them."

"How sad."

"Frightening's more like it," Justyn said. "Paranoia induced by big business."

"He sounds like he went a little nuts," Niccole said.

"That's what I first thought, but a lot of the things he said made sense."

"Like what?"

"Like...Why are the two most beneficial aspects of society, both for the betterment of mankind, the most expensive?" he posed to her.

"What two things?"

"Medicine and education. BC believes both should be free. But the doctors wouldn't want to lose the money or power. And the universities don't want to lose their money or status.

"If you educate the peasants, they're harder to fool. The ruling elite wouldn't want that either. No no no no no," he riveted, BC's lectures running through his head. "Then the battle would really be on."

"What battle?"

"Between the classes. And it wouldn't just be strikes and boycotts, either. It would be fisticuffs and guns."

"What is life about, JT?" she asked.

He scooted towards her and laid a hand on her bare thigh. "Life's about looking into your eyes and kissing those lips," he serenaded. He leaned to her and kissed her cheek.

She broke away and said, "I hear the breakers."

The Cafe

      Niccole and Justyn sat in a booth by a window in a
small cafe on the outskirts of town, the waiter taking their
order. There weren't many patrons but they were all obviously
tourists; all Caucasian with a red tint to their skin. Two men
eyed the mixed couple with blatant disgust from the other side
of the small room.

      "So, being exposed to this BC made you the cynic you
are today?" Niccole started when the waiter had left.

      "I'm not a cynic," Justyn said. "But he did open my
eyes, I guess. The time I spent with the bank didn't help either.
I mean, I read the ads our customers read; I heard the

commercials - We care about you. Then they would tell me to start foreclosure proceedings when customers missed only one payment."

She started to say something but stopped when she saw him tense.

"Those two guys across the way there don't like the idea of us." Justyn emphasized 'idea' to indicate their racial difference.

"How do you know?"

"I heard one of 'em say something when we walked in and they keep looking this way."

"What did they say?"

"I'd rather not repeat it."

"And why not?"

"I'd just rather."

"JT..."

"No. Now, if you'll excuse me, I gotta get rid of that coffee we had on Stoney."

"That's not fair," she shot at him as he stood. He just smiled at her and walked away from the table.

To Justyn's dismay, the restroom was located on the other side of the cafe, near the two men they were just discussing. He sucked in a lungful of air as he neared the table, keeping his gaze straight ahead. As he passed the table he could feel their attention focus on him. Once passed, the smaller of the two spoke,

"Nigger lover."

It was the same phrase Justyn had heard on when he and Niccole entered the cafe. "That's the best he could come up with," Justyn muttered to himself as he disappeared through the restroom entrance.

The little bigot spoke again, this time just to his partner. "C'mon, Billy. Let's go have some fun while the fairy's away."

"Ain't time. He's probably just taking a piss," Billy cautioned his friend. "Forget about 'em, Ned."

"No!" Ned demanded. "We'll take care of the fairy when he comes out. Till then, let's have some fun with his sex slave." Ned stood quickly, skidding his chair back, nearly knocking it over, "Now!" The few customers, and the waiter, turned their attention to Ned. Niccole calmly sipped her water.

Billy rose. "Come on, Ned. Sit down and fin.."

"C'mon, Billy!" Ned barked, then put his hands on the table and leaned close to Billy's face. "No one will stop us," Ned said, then started towards Niccole. Billy followed when he saw the other patrons had returned to their food.

Niccole could feel when the two men approached her. She had been through this before and dreaded the coming confrontation. She knew she would hate the words, their voice, their breath, their eyes. She looked around the cafe, the waiter had disappeared into the kitchen and everyone else was ignoring the situation, their focus on their plates. She turned back to the table and grasped her water glass tightly, but left it on the table.

"Hey bitch!" the little bigot, Ned, hissed when he reached Niccole.

"Do I know you?" Niccole calmly responded without looking at the man.

"You will after I fuck the shit outta ya'," Ned snorted. "You'll get to know me even better when I beat the life outta ya' when I'm through."

"Now why would you want to do that?" Niccole questioned, her voice calm, steady. "What have I done to you to warrant such wrath?"

"You came in the door," Ned accused with blatant hatred. Billy joined Ned then, stepping up and into his role.

"What's the pretty nigger bitch got to say for herself?" he asked Ned while glaring at Niccole.

"She's a smart-ass nigger, Billy. We're gonna have to do her good," Ned said and reached for Niccole.

Niccole responded with the water glass, throwing the water into Ned's face. "Leave me alone," she warned, holding the glass by the bottom now, waiting. Billy stared at Ned, snickering.

"Fucking bitch!!" Ned yelled. "Goddamn fucking nigger-bitch!" and reached for her again. Niccole brought the glass down on his hand, forcing his hand to the table where the glass broke, embedding large pieces into the back of his hand. He jerked it back, screaming in pain as blood spurted out of the wounds.

Billy punched Niccole in the face while she was leaned forward watching Ned. She fell back hard into the booth, blood streaming from her nose and mouth. Billy then reached in and grabbed the front of her blouse, pulling her up out of the booth. Niccole came up like a rag, dazed by the punch, her blouse ripping around the shoulder seams and down the back.

Billy stood Niccole up and held her up. Ned, his left hand numb and bleeding, stepped up and threw his other fist into her abdomen.

Justyn stepped out of the restroom in time to witness

the punch thrown by Ned. His rage was instantaneous. He bolted for Niccole, scooting tables and knocking over meals and chairs as he sprinted across the room. He watched the little bigot strike Niccole two more times before reaching her, the rage inside him growing logarithmically each time.

Justyn reached Ned as he brought his arm back for another swing. Justyn grabbed Ned's arm and continued with the backward motion, stopping only after hearing a sickening crack come from the little bigots shoulder.

Ned screamed in pain and dropped to the floor. Justyn then turned to Ned's partner.

Billy was a bit bigger than Ned. Standing over six feet tall and an easy two-twenty-five, he was nearly twice the size of Justyn's hundred and sixty-eight pound wire frame. Justyn held his ground though, the fury of rage in his eyes.

"Let go of her," Justyn ordered.

Billy did as he was told and let go of Niccole. She slumped to the floor, unconscious. Unable to stop himself, Justyn went to her and stooped over her motionless body.

Billy seized the opportunity and kicked Justyn in the ribs. Justyn fell on top of Niccole, stunned. He felt the big man kick him again, but the pain didn't register. He was too angry to feel pain, but he couldn't breathe, the first kick having knocked the wind out of him. He only saw one thing in his minds eye, though, and that was the big bigot lying next to the little bigot. He felt himself kicked again, keeping him off balance.

"I call police!" a man yelled.

The waiter? The cook? Justyn couldn't tell. And did he call police, or he's going to call them? The large bigot had heard him as well, momentarily relinquishing his kicking practice on Justyn's ribcage. Justyn took the opening, gulping air as he moved.

Still feeling no pain from the beating, his adrenaline pumping, Justyn got quickly to his feet, grabbing the testicles of the large bigot on the way, pulling up.

Billy's eyes shot open to the size of silver dollars. Then his legs buckled beneath him and he fell to his knees, forcing Justyn to release his grip.

Justyn stepped quickly behind Billy and grabbed the big bigot's collar with his left hand. He brought his right hand back, clenched tightly into a fist, then struck Billy at the base of the skull. Billy slumped to the floor next to Ned.

It was some minutes before the island police arrived. When they did, they found two unconscious men and Justyn; sitting on the floor, his back against a table leg, cradling the still unconscious Niccole in his arms.

Aftermath

    Natalie and Jonas were enjoying breakfast on deck
when the patrol boat pulled along side with StoneAge Wizard's
tender lashed to its stern. They both realized there was trouble
when they saw that Niccole was alone. The patrol boat dropped
off Niccole and the tender, informed Jonas that his presence
was requested by the Chief of Police, in one hour, then left
without any further explanation.
    "Rookies," Jonas said, watching the patrol boat pull
away. "I'll have to mention their attitude when I talk to Julio.
    "Now, what happened to you," he said as he stared at
Niccole's black eye, "and where is JT?"

Niccole told Natalie and Jonas about the fight in the cafe and the only reason she was there was because JT had said they were crewing on Stoney. Seems most of the police force knows Jonas, though they did find it difficult to believe that he had a crew. She told them that both men were in the hospital and Justyn had been taken care of by the medic at the jail. All she knew was that Justyn had 'some' cracked ribs. She looked at Jonas when she told them that he had coughed up blood while they were talking through the bars.

"What about you, Sweetheart?" Natalie cooed in a motherly tone. "Your lip and cheek are swollen. And your eye is puffy. Are you hurt anywhere else?"

"I got some bruised ribs, too." She turned to Jonas.

"Cap'n, you gotta get JT outta there. He was only defending me from those animals."

"I'll see what I can do. Something is already wrong here. Julio has a better sense of fairness than this."

Natalie helped Niccole below as Jonas gathered his things for the trip ashore.

*   *   *

Several hours later Niccole awoke to Jonas' voice in the main cabin. She had been napping in the V-berth. He was telling Natalie of the meeting with the Chief of Police.

"This is the kind of shit that keeps me at sea." It was the first time Niccole had heard Jonas swear.

"I can't believe your friend can't do anything," Natalie said.

"It's out of Julio's hands. One of the kids' father knows

93

the governor of the island. Julio says that JT will be released when the two are let out of the hospital," Jonas explained.

"And how long is that suppose to be?"

"A week for the one with the shoulder torn out of its socket. Possibly a month for the one with the concussion. According to the doctor, an inch lower and JT would be up on a murder charge.

Off to Sea the Wizard

      Justyn's stay in the island jail didn't quite last two weeks, but long enough for his bruised ribs to heal. The blood Niccole witnessed him cough up was from an ulcer, another benefit of the bank. The shoulder case was let out in four days - he was the one who's father was a friend of the governor. The concussion case came around in ten days. He made arrangements to have himself transferred State-side two days later: "Away from these primitive aborigines," he sneered at Julio. StoneAge Wizard set sail late that same day.

      They had kept Stoney' in the Gulf Stream all the way from Antigua. Their first landfall after leaving the Caribbean was the south of England. They had run into only four squalls in the eighteen days it took to reach Plymouth, unusual for November.

Now, as they made their way towards the coast of the Netherlands on the eastern horizon, the sea was short and choppy, making the last leg of their passage bumpy and rough.

Jonas was at the helm, his hair whipping about in the twenty knot wind. Natalie was in the cockpit with Jonas, content on being near him and feeling the spray on her face. She was sorry that the passage was coming to an end, but was glad to be getting off the rough sea. She also knew that landfall only made setting sail again that much more wonderful. Too, she wanted to meet this mysterious Rory. Jonas had spoke of him, but never much.

Rory lived in Amsterdam. He moved there fleeing the U.S. What he was fleeing Jonas did not say. He was married to a very special lady and in business of his own.

Justyn and Niccole were below, sleeping. Natalie had wanted to wake them when they could see the coast, but Jonas said to let them sleep.

*   *   *

The sun was setting when the taxi dropped the four off at Rory's. The three story brick house before them sat lengthwise across the lot. A chimney on either end and a bay window centered on the top floor gave the house the appearance of being taller and wider than it actually was. The porch was just to the right of center. Jonas knocked, checked the knob, then walked in and shut the door behind him, leaving the others on the porch to stare at each other.

Natalie and Niccole wondered about Rory and his wife while Justyn examined the street. Long shadows lay across the canal on the other side of the street. The canal lamps were coming on in sequential random. Shadows darkened the cobble stone street, the street lamps illuminating only patches. On the far side of the canal Justyn could see people walking. Small sailboats and wooden launches lined the edges of the canal. A gondola glided silently through the middle of the water, hints of voices seeping to him as Justyn turned to his right. There was no one on the street on this side of the canal. Several blocks down a bridge spanned the canal, linking the two sides. Justyn turned to his left to find the street just as empty. He then looked up. The clear sky fading into night, darkening in shades of blue from west to east. The click of the door latch silenced the women, Justyn turned and faced the door.

Jonas stood in the doorway and beckoned them in. "It's all right," Jonas said. "He's busy in the garden right now, but he'll be right up."

"Right up? From the garden?" Justyn questioned.

"You have got to learn patience, JT. You'll see after dinner. Now come on."

They walked through the door into a large, wood paneled foyer were they removed their jackets and hung them on hooks before entering the main hall. A door was to their immediate right, then a staircase and another door further down. An open door to their left revealed a large, almost empty room. Jonas led the way through the door on the left.

Two windows were in each outer wall. The long room was a quarter size of the house, with two wood frame chairs that faced each other from opposite walls. A small, round, wood frame table sat next to each chair. A small, plush couch and a coffee table on the far wall were the only other furniture in the large room. Jonas invited them to have a seat while they waited for Rory.

Niccole and Natalie sat on the couch, Jonas between them as they waited. Justyn walked to a front window that gave a view of the street and canal and watched the water flow by, immersed in thought.

Concerned about his future, especially now that it looks like Nicci will be in it, he would need to find work. Maybe he could skipper charter boats in the Caribbean. If she danced in one of the clubs, they could save enough for a boat of their own in just a few years. Justyn glanced over to Niccole and kicked himself. Hard. He didn't want her dancing again. Not for any one but himself.

"Evening everyone," boomed a deep voice.

Justyn turned from the window to see a short, stocky man from the same era as Jonas in the doorway. He wore loose fitting khaki trousers, the kind with pockets on the side of the legs. His button down shirt was the same earth colour. Long white hair that was parted down the middle reached below the collar of his shirt. A white caterpillar lay across his upper lip, white sideburns slid down his jawbone like cobwebs, leaving only his chin bare. His round, wire-rimmed glasses reflected the overhead light so Justyn could not see his eyes. "Welcome to Amsterdam, and my home," Rory said as he crossed the room.

Justyn walked towards Rory as Jonas pushed himself off the couch, turning to assist the women.

Rory stared at Justyn as he approached. The description Jonas had provided was uncanny. The man before him was what he had seen in his mind's eye.

"I'm Justyn Thyme," he said with his right hand extended. "JT will do," he added as they clasped hands.

"Rory Tristan," the white caterpillar trembled as he spoke. He shook Justyn's hand twice. "Remarkable," he muttered. "Nice to meet you, Jus'." His voice was baritone, but had a lightness to it.

The image of a large hummingbird, with a white caterpillar on its beak, flew through Justyn's mind. Close, Justyn could see Rory's eyes. They were brown and full of life, the eyes of a child.

"I've heard a lot about you," Rory said.

Justyn looked at him, stupefied.

"Jonas has sent me a few letters. And a phone call from Antigua. Very chivalrous of you." He let go of Justyn's hand and turned to Niccole.

"You must be Niccole," he said, then turned his head back to Justyn. "I can see why you fought for her. I hope your stay in jail wasn't too unpleasant."

Justyn shook his head, mindlessly rubbing his side that was kicked.

"I'm very pleased to meet you, Niccole," Rory said, then took her hand and kissed it.

"So you're Rory," she said, placing the face with the name. "Natalie's told me a little bit about you. We're going to have to talk."

"Of course." Rory then turned to face Natalie. "You must be Natalie." He took her hand and kissed the top of it.

"I'm especially glad to finally meet the woman who has stolen Jonas' heart."

"Uh, thanks," Natalie said. "I like to think that he gave it to me, though," she added, glancing at Jonas. Jonas winked at her.

"I'll except that," Rory said, finally turning to his old friend. "And just how are you, you Old Salt? The sea still being kind to ya'?"

"She's temperamental as always," Jonas said, approaching Rory with his arms wide. "Now give me a hug you, Old Pothead."

Rory and Jonas embraced, slapping each other on the back. Justyn smiled, the genuine affection of the two old friends brought memories of the street and his buddies there.

When the embrace ended, Rory turned to his guests and said, "My home is yours. Now come, I have a stew on the stove simmering."

As the others started towards the door, Rory pulled Jonas back and whispered, "Think he'll do it?"

Jonas shrugged.

Rory's Garden

    The dinner conversation finally got around to Rory's absent wife.

    "Where's Wil'?" Jonas asked.

    "She's down in Breda visiting family. She'll be back in the morning."

    "How'd you meet her?" Natalie prodded.

    "We met in the coffee shop up the street a ways. The funeral home is further up."

    "Hold on," Justyn interrupted. "Funeral home?"

    "She used to work there. She figured she'd meet less people that way. She used to be quite withdrawn.

    "Even though she didn't like meeting people, she liked to go the coffee shops now and again."

    "What's so special about a coffee shop?" Justyn asked.

"They sell the Lady in them here," Rory replied matter-of-factly. Then, as memories swam back into his thoughts, he went on about his wife. "We'd sit there smoking, drinking coffee, eating brownies and talking. It went from there to her being my wife in about eighteen months."

"How romantic," Niccole said.

"Who's the lady?" Justyn asked.

"Marijuana."

"What? In public?"

"It's legal here. To an extent. I'm one of the few who are licensed to sell it to the shops. After we finish here I'll show you my garden."

"In the basement?" Justyn queried.

Rory nodded as he took another bite of food.

*　　　*　　　*

Rory opened the door, reached inside and turned on the light. The wooden stairway going down lit up in a dim, incandescent glow. Rory led the way.

From below came the occasional hiss of compressed air. Rory reached the bottom of the stairs and flicked a switch. The rest of the basement lit up in a green glow. "This is my garden."

Justyn looked around the room, his eyes adjusting quickly to the light. The basement was the size of the house it sat under. One corner was cordoned off into a laundry room, the washer and dryer visible through the open door. Four pillars stood equidistant apart, holding up the floor above. On the cinder brick walls, hung at uneven intervals, were large botanical charts of the only plant growing. "Why green?"

"The plants are in their sleep state. Green doesn't wake 'em up," Rory explained.

Set off in rows of two, running from the front of the house to the back, perpendicular to the stairs, were two foot wide planters, set end-to-end. Sixteen rows ran from one end of the house to the other. They stood a foot off the floor.

The plants closest to the stairs were sown close together. They were tall and thin, nearly all stalk. On the far side of the room were two more rows of the same plants, but they had been planted further apart and were growing bushy and wide.

Each row of planters had high-pressure sodium lamps running the length, six feet apart and a foot above the tallest plant. Black rubber garden hoses and half-inch copper tubing crawled to each box along the rail running between each pair of planters. Along the length of hose and tubing were nozzles pointed over the plants. Justyn figured out the hoses were for watering, but the tubing baffled him. He followed it back to the wall along the laundry room and to three tall, white tanks. The copper tubing originated the from the tanks. The hose went into the room. Justyn let out a quiet whistle, he was looking at an underground greenhouse. They stepped out between the planters, following Rory.

"Your wife's name is Will?" Niccole asked Rory.

"Wilhemina. Her mother named her after the first woman to become queen of Holland. Most everyone calls her Wil." He stopped walking and looked at Jonas. "How long you plan on staying, Jonas?"

"We'll talk about it tomorrow at the loft."

Justyn looked at the back of Jonas' head with crinkled brow. The length of the stay had never been mentioned. It was just, 'We're going to Amsterdam to see Rory'.

"What kind of plants are these?" Justyn asked.

"Marijuana."

"I told you it was legal here," Jonas said.

"Even the scrawny tall ones over here?" Justyn pointed to the left.

"That's hemp. The stalks and seeds are the cash crop there." Rory nodded to his right. "Those over there are being grown to smoke. That's what I sell to the coffee shops. Talk about a cash crop."

"What's with the tanks and tubing?"

"C-O-2. Come on," he gestured with his head. "I'll show you around." As they walked around the basement he pointed out the various strains in the 'for smoke' section and their different stages of growth. He explained the growing time and the affect the amount and color of light had on yield size. He pointed to the copper tubing and hoses on the floor, explaining the influx of carbon dioxide on plant growth and the self-watering system. He boasted a little of his success' with cloning and hand-pollination.

"You must all be tired," Rory said as they arrived back at the stairs. "Let's go back upstairs and I'll show you to your rooms."

"I'd like to hear more about all this," Justyn said.

"Not me," Natalie said. "I'm tired. Jonas and I had a long day." She looked to Jonas, who smiled in agreement.

"I think I'm going to read awhile," Niccole said, smiling a coy smile at Justyn. They headed for the stairs.

Rory made a quick check of the watering system, eyeing the gauges on the carbon dioxide tanks before following his guests up the stairs, turning off the green lights as he left.

The Lady

After walking the others to their rooms on the second floor, Rory led Justyn up another set of stairs to the top floor. Rory turned on the overhead light, illuminating an office. Set askew to the walls were two desks facing each other, a computer atop each. A fax/copy machine was on a stand of its own near the furthest desk, a printer in the far corner. Potted plants were placed about the office, filling empty spaces on file cabinets and bookshelves. They made their way through the office towards the front of the house, and another door.

Rory opened the door and entered the dark room. Justyn, a step behind, stopped at the doorway while Rory crossed into the shadows. An odor of books, old leather, and smoke, drifted by Justyn. Before his eyes had a chance to adjust to the dimness of the canal lights bleeding through the window in the opposite wall, the room flashed bright when Rory struck a match. Justyn stepped into the room as Rory lit a kerosene lamp on a shelf, the rectangular room coming into focus as the light gradually intensified.

They were standing in Rory's den. The wall to the left a few feet away, the one to the right over twenty. Just to Justyn's right and across from him, several steps away, a bay window stretched to the floor, looking out over the canal. Heavy curtains hung at either side. At the far end of the room sat two wing chairs, facing a fireplace. Just to his left was a large, antique, roll-top desk, the top open. It looked old and heavy. A dense, black cloth tall-back chair was cocked his way. By the wear in the seat, it was a well used chair. Bookshelves lined all other wall space.

Rory lit another lamp on another shelf on the wall, then turned to Justyn. "I've been growing and studying the Lady for twenty-five years, Jus'. Smoking it even longer. I can tell you the type of high you'll get by what you smoke and how you smoke it. Here..." Rory turned away from Justyn and stepped to his desk.

"I've never smoked it before," Justyn admitted.

Rory flicked on a small, writing lamp sitting on the desktop, revealing neat stacks of papers and several notebooks. A laptop sat closed on the far end. The pigeon holes in the back were of various sizes and numbered over fifty. He reached into a square hole somewhere around the middle and extracted something that fit in his hand.

"Really??" Rory queried as he returned to Justyn. "Never?"

"Really. It's illegal, you know."

"Not here. Besides, you can smoke it whether it's legal or not." Rory held out his hand to Justyn. "Here."

Justyn looked down to see a black cigarette case open up, the picture on the lid flashing by. Inside were twelve neatly hand-rolled marijuana cigarettes.

"Why smoke?"

"Because of the affect. It's..." Rory paused, searching for the right word, "an enlightenment."

"Really?"

"Really. People have been smoking the Lady for centuries. Using hemp for things even longer.

"Ever try peyote?" Rory quickly queried.

Justyn was taken aback by the question, only because of the deviation from the lecture. He wasn't ready for questions. He blinked a few times, clicked his tongue, then dryly said, "Never even heard of it."

"It's another plant that can do wonders for the mind. But back to the Lady; it's illegal for economic reasons, not because of the high." Rory looked into Justyn's eyes. "Here, let's try something. I've got a feeling." He pointed to one of the joints. "This one here. Sensi Skunk. Good high. Wait. Better in the wee hours, with candles, or outdoors." He looked at Justyn again. "Um, no," he decided, then pointed to another. "This one here. Real nice. Thai. No, not now. Smoke it with Nicci some night, or go for a walk.

"This here is Indica. I think..," his finger brushed over the joints. "Here," he said as he pulled one from the case.

"Northern-Lights." He breathed in its aroma as he held it close to his nose. "Yes," he exhaled. He held the marijuana cigarette out to Justyn. "Jus', I'd like to introduce you to the Lady."

"I-I don't know, Rory," Justyn said apprehensively.

"It's okay, Jus'. There's nothing to worry about."

"I just don't know."

"Why? Because it's illegal back in the 'States?"

Justyn looked at Rory. "And just about everywhere else, too."

Rory lowered the joint to his waist, hooking a finger in a belt loop. "But not here. Here it is legal. You can't get into any trouble if they caught you, but they're not even looking.

"Ever smoke cigarettes?"

Justyn hadn't thought of a cigarette since the Caribbean. "Until recently."

"This stuff is less harmful and a lot more fun than cigarettes."

Justyn glanced towards the door.

Rory picked up an impression. "If Jonas wasn't so tired, he'd be up here with us. I'm not sure about the women."

"An enlightenment?" Justyn queried.

"You'll have to try it to experience it. There's really no way to explain it."

Justyn looked toward the chairs.

Rory watched Justyn ponder the decision. Then raised the joint to Justyn.

"Let me see..." Justyn said as he turned back to Rory, stopping when he saw the joint within easy reach. "Let me see that thing," he said as he took the joint.

"Have a seat, Jus'," Rory pointed to the wing chairs.

"I'm going to make a pot of tea for myself. Would you care for some? Or perhaps something else?"

"Tea will be fine." He held up the joint. "Want me to wait for you?"

"Nope. That one is all yours. Enjoy." Rory stepped to the door. "I'll be back shortly. Have a seat and light up." He opened the door, then turned to Justyn before walking out. "Light the fireplace, too, will you? It's all set, just toss in a match."

Justyn nodded, then walked over to the chairs with joint in hand, examining the bookshelves along the short trip. There were sections on horticulture, botany, mathematics, physics, biology, astronomy, politics, shamanism; literature spanning all genres.

As he approached the fireplace, he noticed a small, oval table setting in front of the chairs. Stepping between the chairs brought him to the table.

A tree branch, cut at an intersection of five branches, was being used for a base. The top was glass. Centered on it was a glass vase with two vines dangling from either side; a hookah. Five candles of different sizes and stages of use were scattered around. A shot glass with wooden matches sat off to the right. He removed a match and stepped to the mantle. He scraped the tip of the match across the stone and it sparked into life. He held it down at an angle to get it burning, then threw it at a wad of paper in the fireplace.

He stepped back to the wing chairs and sat in the one to the left as he faced the growing fire, the leather crunching beneath his weight. He glanced to his right at the table, the water-pipe catching his eye. "Hookah smoking caterpillar," he mumbled, Rory's mustache coming to mind.

As the fire grew, Justyn sat forward and studied the waterpipe, then noticed that the tabletop wasn't clear glass. It was opaque, milky. He tapped his finger on it. It didn't resound with the thunk of glass. He figured acrylic and dismissed it. He grabbed another match and leaned back into the chair.

The overstuffed chair wrapped around his body, molding to him as his weight settled and the leather started to warm. He struck the tip of the match with his thumbnail and it popped into flame. He held the joint up to the light from the match and examined it.

'What am I doing?' he thought. 'I've never smoked this shit before, why should I now? Rory had said to go ahead. It was legal here. But if it was legal here, why was it illegal everywhere else?' Justyn put the joint to his lips, missing a cigarette more than ever before. He put the flame to the joint.

The smoke was cool, sweet. A distant voice told him to hold the smoke in his lungs as long as he could. He inhaled three more times.

He sank further into the chair, the leather softened by body heat. The room imperceptibly grew sharper, the flames from the hearth brighter. A gentle but steady breeze crawled past his ankles. He felt the heat from the fire on his forehead. Then the room swirled, counter-clockwise.

The twist was subtle, but it quickly picked up speed until the swirl became hypnotizing to witness. Justyn focused on the center of the swirl, his body feeling light, almost nonexistent. Suddenly, he wanted Niccole, cuddled on his lap, or cuddled in hers. He closed his eyes and instantly went back aboard StoneAge Wizard, two days before reaching Cape

Horn. . .

. . . he and Niccole were in the cramped crew berth,
moving forward in their romance. They were standing, facing
each other, both without shirts. Justyn was holding her close to
him, panting. Niccole held him tightly, her breath also erratic.
When his breath slowed and hers evened out, he pushed
himself to arms length - looking into her eyes.

"I know this isn't going to come out right. No matter
how I say it. And I know it's going to offend you," he said
softly.

"I think I know what it is," she said, her eyes to the
deck.

"I'm sorry. But I have to ask. I've got this voice inside
my head that keeps bringing it up."

She remained silent, still looking down.

"Natalie told me you never went home with any of the
customers," he said dryly, the doubt hinted at in his tone. "That
doesn't mean you've never had anybody, does it?"

She looked at him, her eyes suddenly hard. She let
loose of him and turned and faced the cabin door. In that
instant he had seen the hurt he caused in her eyes. He reached
for her, intending to take back the question when she moved,
grabbing her discarded shirt and covering herself. Justyn
thought she was going to leave when she stepped towards the
door, but she was just getting some space between them. She
turned to face him. They both grabbed for a handhold as the
boat rolled unexpectedly.

Then, in a tone indicating she wasn't ashamed or sorry
about her past, she said, "I thought I was in love, twice, before
I started dancing. Neither lasted very long. Each time we made

love, it wasn't right. It didn't feel right." Her eyes shifted back and forth as she searched his for his response.

"As for the customers, I danced for them. That was it. None of them ever came home with me. Ever."

Tears were in her eyes as Justyn gazed into them. Still, her voice was firm, strong.

"I was alone a lot, Thyme. A lot." She wiped the tears off her cheek, sniffed, then continued. "I've been alone a long time, dreaming about you, us. And even though I tried, tried my damnedest, I couldn't forget you."

He stood there motionless, his mind totally blank. Except for the realization that he just blew it. Not knowing what else to do, he reached out to her, arms outstretched, beckoning. "I'm sorry," he managed to get out. "I'm an idiot."

She reached back, the shirt diving to the deck. He pulled her close, tight, trying to fuse them together. Trying to let her know that he had fallen in love with her again. Then, in a soft whisper he said, "I love you, Niccole." He felt tears run down his chest and abdomen. She pulled him even closer.

"I've always loved you, JT". . .

Rory re-entered the room. Justyn had let the joint go out between his fingers, half smoked. His mind was whirling and didn't hear Rory until the door clicked shut. He looked at the clock on the mantle and marveled at how the time did not coincide with what he felt passed. Twenty minutes by the clock, several hours in his mind.

Justyn sat forward slowly, unsure of what just happened to him. He had never had memories return like that before. Not that vivid. He glanced down to see if he had a shirt on - he did. An erection, too. He rolled his head to look at

Rory.

"Oh, you're back," he said, his voice coarse and low, then leaned back. His mind was operating on several levels at once, separate realms each. "Fires lit."

"I can see that. Thanks for lighting it." Rory put the tray down on the coffee table and sat on the edge of the other chair. On the tray was a small pot, warmed by a votive candle, two cups, sugar, cream, honey, spoons, and a variety of teabags in a wide, thick, squatty glass.

Rory removed a match from the shot glass on the table and lit it off the votive under the teapot. He then lit the candles on the table, placing the spent match on the tray.

"Here, take your pick of teas and prepare as you like," Rory said. He placed a teabag in a cup for himself, then poured in hot water.

"Just...in...time," Rory mumbled as he clanked the teapot onto the tray. It was nearly inaudible over the clank. Justyn only heard the tone of Rory's voice.

"Pardon?"

"Are you high?" Rory asked.

"I think so. I'm definitely relaxed. Very...happy." He spoke in a sedated tone; slow, with elongated pauses between phrases. "Almost like sailing."

"Euphoria," Rory stated. Then asked, "You've never smoked before?"

Justyn thought a moment. "Nope. Never."

"You're sure," Rory insisted. "Not even a joint when you turned thirty?"

"No," Justyn said. "And what's so special about thirty?"

Rory shrugged.

"Why the interrogation warden?"

"You sure you're high?" Rory repeated.

"I think so. Now why so many questions?" Justyn asked back.

"The Lady must like you. I had a feeling. So did Jonas."

"What the hell are you talking about?" Justyn's confusion was obvious.

"Like I said, I just thought you'd like it."

Justyn sat still for a moment, then sat forward to retrieve a match. He sank back into the chair before lighting the dormant joint. As he exhaled he asked again, "What are you talking about?"

"How much do you know about marijuana?" Rory asked.

"Mmm-m-m-m, not much really. I do know I'm beginning to like it. It tastes better than cigarettes." He smiled, a tight-lipped grin that squished his cheeks into his eyes. Rory smiled back.

"Why? What's going on? You seem to know the affects of this stuff. And why do you call it the 'Lady'?" Justyn scooted to the edge of his chair, leaning towards Rory. He put the joint on the tray and made himself a cup of tea. Chamomile.

Rory sank into his chair, fading into it's shadows.

"Ya see, Jus', marijuana has been in use for thousands of years. And not just for the high." His voice seemed to emanate from the chair itself. "But it's uses have been lost in the hype over the high that really isn't harmful.

"And it's the high that can open doors. Doors to

creativity and imagination. Take you on terrific journeys to other worlds and physical planes.

"Today's world is just too busy. Busy doing nothing."

Rory took a sip of his tea, Justyn took another hit. Rory continued.

"Along time ago I knew this woman, Denise. She took me on journeys that really changed things for me." Rory's tone had become serious, demanding Justyn to listen. "She took me to the desert for four days once. We fasted a day and a half to cleanse our bodies.

"Then, the third night, as we sat by the fire and watched the stars go by, she loaded the small bowl of a long, narrow pipe with the Lady and a few other herbs, then gave it to me. I took two hits and started to put it down. I was feeling really good with only the two hits in me. Whatever it all was, it was some good shit.

"'Cept, she wouldn't let me stop. She pushed the pipe back up to my mouth, telling me to smoke it all. I waited some seconds before lighting it again.

"When I finally tapped out the ashes some minutes later, she told me to close my eyes. I did."

Justyn closed his eyes. He saw the campfire, his view from above and behind. Two figures, sitting cross-legged and close together, sat near the fire.

"As soon as I closed my eyes she was beside me and we were going up, up into the sky. I looked down and saw both of us as we just were, still sitting by the fire. Absolutely motionless. I began to ask what, but she answered in my head as the question formed. We were going to other worlds. I squeezed her hand tight."

"Hunh?" Justyn muttered, eyes still closed. He was trailing the two on their flight, above and behind.

"We were having an out of body experience, Jus'. Astral projection. We flew past the Moon, Mars, Jupiter, out of our solar system. We passed the Oort Cloud and went on to other galaxies."

Justyn opened his eyes and glanced quickly around the room, making sure he was still in Amsterdam.

"I tell ya', Jus', approaching a spiral galaxy face on is a sight to behold. I only wish I could paint. Even then I don't think I could do justice to the beauty that's out there in the silence."

Justyn reached forward and picked up his tea by the saucer, then leaned back into the shadows and security of the chair. Why did all this seem to have some truth to it? He should be rolling with laughter, out of the chair and onto the floor. Or perhaps he should be bolting for the door. A plant that sends you on astral journeys, out of body experiences, trips to other galaxies.

Silly.

'Til he remembered that little trip he took back in time himself just moments before, and the one with Rory just now. And if he could somehow separate the words from Rory's voice.

Here, in the dancing glow of fire, the aroma of kerosene and weed, Rory's baritone voice hovered in the shadows, each word charged with an energy of its own, the inflections and the tones emphasizing concepts. Justyn wondered briefly if it was the marijuana causing the depth of his perceptions, then dismissed it without reason. Still though, there was a twinge of doubt to what Rory said. This stuff is illegal nearly everywhere else.

"I didn't know marijuana caused hallucinations?" Justyn said. He had heard about marijuana, but nothing like this.

"No, Jus', it wasn't a hallucination," Rory explained. "Well, maybe it was. But who's to say what hallucinations really are. Places we don't normally go, perhaps? And because not everyone sees it, those that do are nuts and are seeing things? Besides, there were other herbs in the pipe."

Justyn didn't respond. His mind was spinning at the things he had just heard, the visions he witnessed just moments ago. He jumped when Rory spoke again, the teacup rattling on the saucer.

"When I found out that marijuana used to be legal in the States, I had to find out why it was made illegal. What I found angered me. Pissed me off.

"I discovered the Lady has a variety of beneficial uses, and the reasons why she's not being put to those uses." Rory leaned toward Justyn, as if to whisper a secret. "It's all economical. Monopolies. Conspiracies. That sort of thing."

"You called it the Lady again," Justyn interrupted. "Why do you call this stuff the Lady?"

"One of the nicknames for marijuana is Mary Jane. To me, it seemed to fit. I think about it in a feminine way. Almost as a person. Mary Jane Sativa, the gentle Lady of the smoke."

Justyn merely said, "Oh."

"Anyway, I started writing letters to congressmen, to the papers, to any magazine or publication I thought would publish my letters on re-legalization. They started to watch me after a few letters were published, following me. They stopped me on the streets and searched me. I had to quit smoking so they couldn't harass me about that."

"Who followed you, Rory? I hear this stuff makes you paranoid."

"It makes you paranoid because it's illegal. And it was the FBI following me. They showed me their badges a few times."

"What did you say in those letters?" Justyn sounded astonished.

"I guess they got all riled up because I called the government a bunch of liars and cowards. I also said that they really didn't care about the rest of us or the planet, they had it made and that was all there was to it.

"I had to eventually quit writing letters. I even moved. First across town, then to a different state. That's when they killed Denise." Rory paused and sipped at his tea. "That's when I left the good ol' U S of A; with the help of our mutual friend."

"Jonas?"

Rory nodded.

"I'm sorry about your friend," Justyn said quietly.

Rory leaned forward and picked up the joint from the serving tray. He re-lit it, inhaled deeply, then leaned back, handing the joint to Justyn before getting out of reach.

"It's okay, Jus'," he said through his teeth. "It was a long time ago."

"Yeah," Justyn said, "I can hear how long in your voice."

Rory exhaled. "They couldn't get to me, so they tried through her. She wouldn't tell them where I was, so they killed her," Rory said, the emotion choking him a bit. After a moments pause, he barked, "Hell, she couldn't tell them where I was!" Then quieter, "I didn't tell her. I thought I was protecting her that way. But they killed her anyway," he said with a helplessness that showed he still harbored feelings for her.

Rory fell silent, lost in the shadows and folds of the chair. Lost in the past. Justyn sipped at his tea between hits off the joint.

The Economics of Hemp

        Justyn's tea was almost gone. They had been silent for
a little more than an hour. Justyn stared at the fire; the flames
were quick but the burn was slow and dying down. His mind
whirled through memories of his ancient past: Grade school
and the summers between, junior high and meeting Niccole, the
odd jobs after running away from home, sailing the Caribbean
Sea, the bank, Sally. Justyn raised the cup to his lips and sipped
the cool liquid. Instantly he spit the tea back into the cup.
        "What's wrong?" Rory asked as Justyn sat forward,
Justyn placing his cup on the table as he searched for another
teabag.

"Cold." Justyn handed the remnant of the joint to Rory. "We gonna light it back up?"

Rory leaned forward and took the joint. He looked at it for a moment then said, "Nope. I'll get another. Hold tight."

Before Justyn realized Rory had left, he was back with a fresh joint. He lit it and handed it to Justyn. "Twenty-five years ago, Jus', I started my own little garden here in Amsterdam. I wasn't living here then. I started growing because I could barely afford to buy any. I had no intentions of selling it. It was to be my own little stock, ya know.

"Anyway, as I waited for my garden to grow, I visited the coffee shops about once a week; to smoke, mostly, but I began reading the material they had on their shelves. Quite a lot of it dealt with the Lady. That, in turn, led me to the museum they have for it here. I've spent a lot of time there." Rory nodded at Justyn. "We'll go there."

Justyn held the joint back out to Rory. Rory declined with a wave of his hand. Justyn withdrew and inhaled again.

"After reading further about the uses of the Lady," Rory continued. "I wanted to get some empirical knowledge. So I planted more seeds; a hundred in all."

"All indoors?"

"No. I didn't start that 'til moving here."

"How come?"

"How come, what?"

"How come indoors? Isn't the sun better for them?"

"Sure, but the growing season here is just too short. Besides, there are no cloudy days in my garden." Rory scooted to the edge of his chair and prepared himself another cup of tea.

"They don't get as tall," Rory sat back, teacup in hand.

"But I get four harvests a year. I can also control the environment indoors, but I told you that in the basement. My outdoor garden gives me one harvest a year."

Justyn nodded with a slight "hmph" of acknowledgment.

Rory sipped, collecting memories of years past. Justyn sat motionless, the joint idling out, his tea cooling, and his mind expanding into the darkness that reigns behind the eyes.

"After my first harvest of hemp I found a factory that would make me some fabric from the stalks. The first batch came out a heavy canvas. I use it for a tarp in my outdoor garden.

"After another harvest and some more trial and error, the factory made some cloth comparable to cotton." He tugged at his shirt, then pants. "Most of mine and Wil's clothes are made of hemp now. All the linen in the house is. The oil burning in the lamps behind us is hemp oil.

"The factory that made the first cloth for me also processes the seeds. They purchase plants from me on a regular basis. They sell the cloth to local manufacturers who make it into clothes." Rory sipped more of his tea.

"Oh, I also have another garden in a warehouse across the city. It's three times as large as the one downstairs. The plants really get tall there." Rory looked to the fire and snatched a quick sip of tea.

"Don't know how I forgot that? Yes I do," he said as he sat back, turning his head to Justyn. "I have a manager there. I visit every couple, three months.

"There's still only the one factory processing the stalks and the demand for the finished product isn't that high yet, but there's enough to keep me busy tending to my gardens.

"Some of the bud from those crops I give to the university to do medical research with."

"Bud?"

"The flower. Ghanja. That's what you smoke of the plant. But the bud from hemp is worthless to smoke. It has less than one percent THC. The short, bushy plants you saw downstairs are for smoking.

"Anyway, now that you've tried it and are high," Rory looked at Justyn, "do you think it should be illegal?"

Justyn shrugged, bringing the teacup to his lips in the same movement.

"The reason it was banned, Jus', wasn't because of the high, but because of economic competition." Rory sat forward, resting his elbows on his knees, his hands out front holding the cup. "Back in the thirties a machine was invented to make hemp production faster, and with less labor so there'd be more profit. Decorticators, they're called." He sipped some tea, then added, "I've got word out that I'm looking for one.

"Anyway, before these decorticators, all the work was done by nature and hand. But with these new machines to break up and separate the plant, mass production of hemp was possible. It became economically viable. They could make a profit.

"The plant was worthless to them, even though it's versatile and biodegradable, until they could get a bigger profit. And people wonder what's wrong with us. We do things for the wrong reason.

"Some of hemp's competition," Rory paused, thinking. "A couple of tycoons; one with a newspaper and paper mills.

The other was into petro-chemicals. Both had products that could be produced with less damage to the environment, just as good, and now, cheaper, using hemp. They became worried about their profits. Maybe people wouldn't buy their products at all. So they lied about one of the most beneficial plants to man and the planet he lives on, made it illegal to grow so they could get rich." Rory's voice dropped to a whisper, Justyn barely hearing what he said next, "They lied, at the expense of the planet and Man's evolution."

"What?" Justyn was expecting a simple repeat of what was said, not,

"Don't you see? They lied. Lied." The tone of voice was of suppressed anger. The kind of anger that makes you more than mad, it causes you to become pissed. "At the cost of this beautiful planet, they lied. They've known all along that hemp could be used for nearly all petroleum products. They knew! Yet, to keep control, to stay the wealthiest, to stay special, they lied.

"It makes no sense, really. They made something illegal that can do everything oil can do and is renewable, and instead use something that is finite and a poison to everything it touches; including men's minds."

Justyn re-lit the joint, his mind entering an unknown realm. He wondered what made this man so passionate about fancy tobacco. He passed the remainder of the joint to Rory.

Rory took it between his fingers and let it go out, his arm on the arm of the chair. After several minutes of silence Rory said, "Sorry for getting so, intense. But if we put this plant to all of its uses, it could save the world. We're killing this planet, Jus'. Do you realize that?"

"How is hemp going to save the world?" Justyn asked. "Not as long as man is alive can this world be saved."

"Damn. And I thought I was cynical," Rory said. "But if we really started using hemp, we can stop cutting down the rain forests, first off. Hemp can be made into nearly everything a tree can, including boards."

Justyn gave Rory a puzzled look he couldn't see and a "Hmm?"

"Fiber boards," Rory said as he re-lit the joint, then handed it to Justyn . "And it was used to make paper well into the late 1800's. Think of it, an annually renewable paper source. Know how many trees that is?" Justyn shook his head. "Damn. Use to know that number. It's a crapload.

"Hemp is also stronger, softer, warmer and more water absorbent than cotton. Yet cotton is used extensively throughout the world now, at a cost to the soil and water from herbicides and pesticides that hemp cultivation doesn't need.

"Christ, Jus', it can be used to make almost anything we make synthetically now. And synthetics aren't biodegradable.

"It can, and has been, used for medicine and food. The bread you had tonight was made from hempseed flour. And we only use hempseed cooking oil. And it's healthy, even the oil. It's one of those Omega-3 things." He took a breath, then went on.

"Hemp can be used to replace fossil fuels. Again, annually renewable. And we could still drive our internal combustion death traps. The infrastructure is already there, it just needs to be cleaned out and tweaked.

"In fact," Rory leaned over the arm of the chair

towards Justyn, then continued in a whisper, as if telling a secret, "I have a large interest in a company in Canada that is making hemp diesel fuel; H2K. They're installing the pumps this year across the country and have a trucking company waiting to use them. The oil companies won't have a chance after that's started." He slid back into the seat, speaking again at a normal tone.

"Um, it can be used to make plastic, paint. Oh geez, this list is so long. I forget 'em all. I've got a paper in the desk with all of it's uses."

Justyn listened, the words racing through his mind, ideas slowly forming. "This is all a bit much for just one plant, isn't it?" he questioned Rory. "Aren't you just saying all these good things about it so you can smoke it? I mean, come on."

Rory sank into the depth of the chair and the shadows. "I *can* smoke it. Legally. Here. And besides, even with it being illegal, people all over the world continue to smoke it."

Justyn realized he held the joint and offered it to Rory. He waved it off so Justyn took another hit.

"And like I said before, the industrial stuff isn't worth squat to smoke."

"But really," Justyn exhaled. "How can a single plant save the world?"

"Haven't you been listening?" Rory said with disappointment. "We can stop polluting the world with oil and synthetics. We can stop cutting down the forests.

"Christ, Jus', people have been using hemp, marijuana, weed, pot, ghanja, Mary Jane, reefer, grass, cannabis," he paused to catch his breath, "for centuries. It's been used for food, clothing, lighting, sails," he paused and leaned towards

Justyn, "the high.

"But a smear campaign was waged against it, using public stupidity and racism to get the plant made illegal. And not because of the high, but to rid economic competition." Rory looked to the floor between his feet and spoke to himself, "Hmph..mankind, and I'm related." He then snapped up from the chair in one motion, saying after he was standing, "It's all really rather sad and disgusting. I think I'll get another joint." He walked back to the roll top desk, returning a minute later with the cigarette case.

Justyn saw the picture on the lid this time; a medieval wizard was smoking from a large kalian. A full moon framed the image against the black of the case.

"This table is made from weed, Jus'," Rory said as he sat back down in the chair. "I know someone down in Breda; he lives fairly close to Wil's parents, in fact. Anyway, I took him some stalks and asked if he could make plastic with it." Rory tapped on the table top. "This is the first result."

Justyn sat forward, scooting to the edge of the chair and stared at the table. After a few moments he reached out and tapped it himself. "Neat."

"Real neat." Rory lit a fresh joint. He inhaled deeply, holding the smoke in his lungs. He sat back in the chair, disappearing again into the shadows.

"How ya' feeling, Jus'?" he said as he exhaled.

"Quiet, but my brain seems to be zooming around like mad. Yet, time seems to be...floating."

"That's the smoke." He drew on the joint again. Justyn could see the glow.

"Want some more?" Rory asked. His voice was

strained. Justyn realized he had spoken while losing little smoke.

"I still have the other one."

"You smoke that and I'll smoke this, then."

"I'm kinda sleepy now."

"There's a group in Jamaica that smokes this stuff daily and there's been no recorded death related to it," Rory stated. "In fact, there's been no recorded case of lung cancer either, and they live as long as non-smokers."

Justyn yawned, then re-lit his joint.

"Don't you see? All the hype about this is just that - hype! Lies." He handed the joint to Justyn. "Trade."

Justyn took the joint, passing the one he held to Rory. When he exhaled, he said, "Hey, this is different from the other one."

"Yah, more potent. You won't be much to talk with pretty soon. I'll take you downstairs before we finish it."

As they passed the joints back and forth, Rory continued his assault on the world.

"The industrial revolution was the worst thing that could have happened to mankind. It was bad enough that our ancestors thought it was right to wipe out entire civilizations just because they wanted their land; just because they didn't like the way they looked or thought. But then to waste the natural resources in the name of business and profit is simply insane. How much of the world lies in landfills and garbage dumps?"

Justyn shrugged, "I dunno."

"Me neither," Rory admitted. "It was rhetorical. But

I've seen a lot of waste in my lifetime. A lot. And for what? For what??"

Justyn shrugged.

"So someone can make a profit," Rory answered his own question, then inhaled from the joint again. There was silence as he held the smoke.

"Things need to change, Jus'. There's too much still wrong with humanity for us to go on the way we are."

Justyn looked at him through purple eyes. Rory reminded him a little of BC.

"Sometimes, Jus', I'm ashamed to be a part of the human race. Everywhere I look I seem to see nothing but stupidity."

"Come on, Rory," Justyn finally said. "Aren't you being just a little harsh? I mean, I don't really like the way things are, either. But.."

"Maybe. Maybe," Rory interrupted. "But not a whole lot has changed in the last two thousand years. People still hate each other because of their color or belief. People are still spouting off about growth and productivity in a finite world. People are still depending on technology to save them and the world. Politicians are still lying to the citizens they're suppose to be serving. Life has become a game of economics. And only for those already rich. The game now is to see how much they can take from every one else. Life has become," he paused, searching for the word, "artificial.

"And it's all because people want it all. But they don't know what they want. They think possessions and materialism is the key to happiness. Hell, why not?!" Rory thrust an arm into the air, his voice rising in volume as he spoke. "The T.V.

tells them that's what they want. They don't realize that what you take into the next world is what you carry inside you, not what you've purchased." Rory paused, the sudden silence thundering in the dim, natural light. "And it counts on how you treated Mother Earth."

It took a few moments for Justyn to reply. When he did, his voice was soft, slow. "Uh, yeah. I'm really tired." He leaned forward to rise, then said, "I just want to fold into Nicci and fall asleep."

"C'mon, Jus'," Rory said. "Let's go downstairs."

Wilhemina's Kitchen

The next morning Justyn awoke to a dry mouth and an empty bed as the sun was nearing its midday apex. The small, cozy room was bright. He rose on the window side. The view out was of the house next door, but if he pressed his face against the glass he could see a narrow slice of the street out front.

The furniture was dark and antique. Justyn would find out later that some of it was handed down from Wilhemina's side of the family from as far back as the mid-1600's.

A door on the far wall led to the bathroom; a toilet, sink and small, square shower. Beside the bathroom, a closet.

Justyn looked at the clock on the nightstand, it was after eleven. He drug his feet towards the shower.

After searching the upper floors and finding no one, Justyn was beginning to think he had the house to himself until he neared the bottom of the stairs and heard the laughter of women coming from the kitchen. He entered the kitchen, the warmth from the fireplace pushing by him with the aroma of coffee enticing him.

He found Niccole and Natalie in the kitchen, a strange woman with them. This, presumably, was Wilhemina. The three of them were sitting around a round, blond wooden table near the fireplace, each with a cup.

"Morning, Night Owl," Niccole said to Justyn. She got up and met him halfway, kissing him on the cheek. She then turned, her arm around his waist and introduced him to Rory's wife. "Wil, this is my man, JT. JT, Wil."

Wilhemina rose to meet the couple. She wore a pleated skirt that brushed her ankles; a thick, colorful, bright, floral print fabric. Large furry slippers covered otherwise bare feet. An oversized, open, baby blue sweater covered a plain white blouse, the top four buttons of the blouse open. Her strawberry hair hung down loosely, some resting on her shoulders, the rest fallen down her back. She was quite pretty, her large breasts increasing her femininity. As she got closer, Justyn noticed her clear, blue eyes. An opalesce blue that flickered and rolled with every movement and shadow. They were the sort that looked through you.

"Good morning, JT," she said, her Dutch accent fitting her aura. "And please, do call me Wil. Every one does, even Mom and Pop."

"Morning, Wil," Justyn said coarsely. His mouth felt as though it had been wiped dry. He forced a swallow.

"I see you've been talking with Rory by the hour i'tis. He's bit eccentric, but I think that's why I love him so."

"Is he around?" Justyn asked.

"Nah, he and Jonas went looking at the loft early this morning. They should be back around lunch," Wilhemina said, then looked at the clock. "Which shouldn't be too much longer. Do you wish to wait for lunch, or would you like breakfast?"

"I'll just have some coffee," he said slowly.

"I'll get it," Niccole said, letting go of him as she went to the counter.

Justyn followed Wil back to the table. "May I join you ladies?" he said as he pulled out the chair nearest the fire and sat down. Wilhemina sat down facing Justyn as Natalie nodded into her cup. The fireplace was brick, an arch footprint that came out from the wall and stretched into the room. On the other side of the fireplace was a pantry, quite large, and a laundry room. But on this side, the kitchen reached to the outer wall.

Natalie sat facing the windows, her back to the wall and the rest of the house. Justyn could see the two doorways into the kitchen behind Wilhemina.

"Thanks, Nic," Justyn said when Niccole placed the cup of black coffee in front of him. He looked up to her, into her capturing green eyes. She gave him a quick kiss on the lips and sat down on his left, windows behind her.

After taking a sip of coffee, Justyn looked back at Wilhemina. "I've got some questions to ask Rory. He put a lot of ideas into my head last night." He paused as he took another sip, then added, "A lot." He drank some more coffee, the first sip doing little to moisten the dryness in his mouth.

"So how do you like smoking the Lady?" Wilhemina asked him.

"Except for some cottonmouth," Justyn said, setting the cup back down, "not bad. I do feel a little sluggish." He turned to Niccole, "What time did I come to bed?"

"You cuddled up next to me at about three in the morning," she said. "Don't worry, Love, you got your eight hours."

He smiled and laid his hand on hers. He squeezed it gently. "You ashamed of me?" he asked quietly.

"What on earth for?" Niccole said in mild surprise. "For smoking pot?"

He nodded, eyes to the table. "And liking it."

She turned her hand in his then squeezed back. Justyn looked up, meeting her eyes. "Of course not. I would think there's something wrong with you if you didn't like it. There's nothing wrong with smoking pot. Besides, I hear you're in good company with Rory."

"He's an herbologist," Wilhemina said. "Also a shaman."

"Why doesn't that surprise me," Justyn said rhetorically, the books in the den flashing through his mind.

"You know about shamans," Natalie remarked in feigned shock.

Justyn pulled the cup from his lips. "Had an uncle that was one. Weird guy."

"Do you think Rory is weird?" Natalie probed.

Justyn was about to say something when they heard the

front door slam shut. The three looked to Wilhemina.

"They're home," she said as she stood, then headed out the kitchen through the nearest doorway. A moment later Jonas walked through the same doorway, still unbuttoning his jacket. Wilhemina and Rory were only steps behind.

"Just getting up?" Rory commented jokingly to Justyn. "How does Jonas put up with that?"

Justyn looked to Jonas, who was now standing behind Natalie, then to Rory, "I stand the night watch on Stoney."

Justyn Thyme, the Hemp Messiah

Lunch was Wilhemina's family stew and more hempseed bread. The women went over plans for their shopping excursion while they ate. Rory and Jonas reviewed their excursion that morning. Justyn listened to everybody a little each as he quietly devoured two bowls of stew.

After lunch the women went out, leaving the men to clean up. Rory and Jonas volunteered for kitchen duty. Justyn was volunteered to clear the dining table. Rory told Justyn he could go to the den and light one up while they did dishes. Justyn accepted.

The thick drapes were drawn tight, not a sliver a light shown through. The room was almost as dark as the night before, but Justyn could see well enough to find his way around without turning on any light.

He found the black case with the wizard on the desk. He grabbed it and went to the chairs. After placing the case on the hemp table, Justyn started a fire. He picked up the shot glass of matches and set them down on the edge of the table nearest the left hand chair, facing the fire. He picked up the case and sat down, the chair seeming to remember him.

He lit one candle when he started the fire, which was growing slowly. He thought he might have to poke it again. What little light there was was absorbed by the books. Justyn sat barely out of darkness. Randomly he selected a joint, then returned the case to the table, retrieving a match on the way back.

Given to the cloak of the chair, Justyn lit the joint and inhaled deeply. He missed Niccole. Any time away from her now was near agony. She made him whole. He took another hit and remembered the way she snores as she sleeps. A small snore. Cute, if it didn't keep him awake. He thought he would be use to by now, but they have been sleeping in the same bunk now for months.

He exhaled and thought perhaps it was all him. Afraid something is going to happen to end his happiness. How his fixation on her snoring was related to that, he didn't know. It didn't matter. He would resolve to enjoy the day, now, each moment. Carpe diem. He took another hit and decided that Nicci's snoring was cute. He really did love her. And her snoring was cute. Soothing, like those noise machines.

He exhaled and smiled at his thoughts. "Nicci, my own living, breathing, white noise machine," he mumbled, his smile broadening.

He took another hit and went sailing with Niccole in a

Caribbean Sunrise Charter boat. One of the company's larger sloops, it clipped along at hull speed and a hard heel. The wind was blowing spray and wavelets into their faces, soaking their upper bodies with luke warm water. Land-fall was up ahead, but he didn't know what land it was. The sky and sea were blue, blending into an indigo haze at the horizon. His impression was this was their island.

He knew he was dreaming then and let the joint go out. He closed his eyes and waited for the sound of the door while his thoughts drifted.

Some minutes later Rory and Jonas entered the room. Rory sat the tea tray down on the table and stepped back to the mantle, a cup in hand, the fireplace kicking to life behind him. Jonas sat in the other chair, the crunching leather audible to the room. Rory looked at Justyn; he was watching the fire. Rory turned to Jonas. Jonas nodded. Rory turned back to Justyn. "Jus'," he paused, waiting for Justyn to look up. "We'd like you to go into politics."

Justyn burst out with laughter. Rory and Jonas only looked at him, their faces solemn. He checked his laughter with a cough. "You can't be serious?" It was rhetorical, but Rory and Jonas both nodded their heads.

"What else have you got to do, JT?" Jonas asked.

"Wha'd'ya mean, 'what else I got to do'?" Justyn retorted. "That doesn't make me the ideal candidate because you two think I don't have anything better to do."

"You've been bitching and moaning the whole way here about how the world needs changing," Jonas said, "now's your opportunity."

"That's just it. I want to get away from all the bullshit.

Permanently. Now you want me to get into politics?!" Justyn stood. "I can't believe it. The worst part of that society and you want me to get into it." He rose from the chair and went to the window. The voice from the shadows of his mind whispered, 'You want to help? Help now'. Justyn turned back to the fire, the moment surreal.

"So, what's this suppose to prove?" Justyn asked.

"It's not to prove anything," Rory stated.

"So, what's the point?"

"It's time to educate the masses. It's time to start changing the world."

Justyn turned back to the window. Change the world. Educate the masses. The asses. How can one man change the world? Me? Change the world? He spoke to the window, but loud enough for the room to hear. "How?"

"If you'll sit back down, I'll explain," Rory said.

Justyn settled back into the chair. It remembered his form. He crossed his arms and ankles, then said, "Okay. Explain."

"Having you run for office with the legalization of the Lady as your platform is the best we can do right now," Rory started, only to be interrupted by Justyn.

"Best you can do what?"

"The best we can do on getting people to re-think their lives, starting with the fuel they put in their cars, the clothes they wear, the food they eat," Rory continued. "It's more than just getting the Lady legalized and using her for everything we possibly can. It's about getting people to realize the harm of consumerism to the planet, everyone's home. It's about enlightenment, Jus'."

"Couldn't we just write letters or books or something? Stay here and smoke. Maybe expand your gardens and the cloth exports. Advertise. Marketing. Not politics."

"You really think the status quo will let the hemp industry survive without support from the government?" Jonas stated in a tone that indicated he didn't. "Do you know how far they would go to stop the manufacturing of hemp products? It's either this or revolution."

"You don't want global anarchy, do you Jus'?" Rory asked.

Justyn stared into the growing fire, its motion calming his mind. His gaze remained on the fire as he asked Jonas, "Won't the status quo try to put a stop to whatever we're doing?"

Jonas shifted his eyes to Rory. "We don't think so," Rory said. "It's too public."

"It would be sacrilegious!" Jonas declared.

"They've done it before," Justyn said dryly. He leaned forward and made himself a cup of tea. He looked up to Rory, "What did you have in mind?"

"With the beard you've got and your facial features," Rory tilted his head to see the side of Justyn's head, "and a little longer hair, you'll have a strong resemblance to Jesus Christ. You'll run as the Hemp Messiah."

"What?!?" Justyn exclaimed. "Run for what?"

"Justyn Thyme for Governor, the Hemp Messiah" Jonas said. "I thought it was catchy."

"You thought it was catchy?" Justyn snipped. Then, a bit more subdued, he asked in general, "Governor of what?" He scooted back into the chair and sipped at the cup.

"California," Jonas said, his belief in the idea obvious in his tone.

"California already has lax marijuana laws," Rory said. "You running with it on your platform won't shock people as much. We'll get you into the Green Party. My friends are semi-", he rocked his hand, palm down, several times, "influential in that party. If nothing else for them, it will get attention drawn to their party."

"Yeah, the kind they don't want." Justyn was looking to the floor, mumbling. Flashes of last night giving "Green Party" a new meaning. "You're more of a Hemp Messiah than I am, Rory. Why don't you run?"

Rory stared at Justyn, shocked at the suggestion.

Justyn looked up after no response. Rory had a hurt look in his eyes. The conversation from last night slipped into his mind. Rory couldn't run for Governor, he couldn't even set foot back in the States. "I'm sorry, Rory. I didn't think before popping off. I know you can't," Justyn looked over at Jonas. "He's got the features of Christ, too. You could use him." Justyn pointed with a nod at Jonas.

"I can't," Jonas boasted. "I'm your campaign manager."

"It's more than that," Rory clarified, turning to look at Justyn. "You've got more charisma than he does." Rory felt Jonas' eyes, but didn't look his direction.

Justyn smiled. He liked Rory. "I don't know anything about politics. Besides, I'm not that good of a liar."

"Who's asking you to lie? You'll be telling the truth about the Lady. You just need to study up on the plant and practice talking to crowds."

"Uh-uh. No way am I getting up in front of a bunch of

142

strangers and give a speech."

"And answer questions," Jonas added.

"Oh, Christ. Campaigning. Nope. Count me out. Ain't no way I can do this. I hate people."

Jonas looked to Rory. "I can vouch for that."

"Has to make it difficult, doesn't he?"

Jonas nodded. Justyn shrugged. "I just don't see the point. I've got no experience. A crappy background. An exotic dancer for a girlfriend. What's the point?"

Rory stepped over and took the joint from Justyn. He stepped back to the fire, reached in and pulled out a small, hot branch to light the joint, tossing the branch back into the fire as he inhaled. "We don't expect you to win, Jus'. But the attempt will show people we're serious. It will start the education of the masses."

"The asses," Justyn said under his breath, then, at normal volume, "And some of those asses will go looking for dirt and an ex-topless dancer is something they'll go apeshit over. I've grown rather fond of her, I won't have her put through that. Besides, I don't think she really has the past for a governor's wife. Hell, I don't really have the past for a governor.

"I have no idea what they'll do with the race difference. I imagine they'll leave it alone for fear of looking racist themselves."

"I can get her, and you, a past," Rory said bluntly.

"There'll be no need for that, Rory," Jonas said. "What JT said is right. They'll for the most part leave her alone. Legalizing marijuana as his ticket will give them enough to talk about."

"All the more reason to play it safe. With that as his ticket, they'll go looking even harder."

"Then the answer is no. I will not put Nicci through that."

"I can get you both history's you'll be proud of."

Justyn looked at Jonas. "What kind of people does he know?"

"The same kind they know."

"Better safe than sorry," Rory stated.

"There's got to be some other way. I can't lie for shit 'cause I hate it so much. I couldn't keep up with a lie about myself, or Nicci's."

"You running for office is about the best thing we can do," Rory laced the sentence with excitement. "Think of the exposure, the publicity for hemp."

"That's what I was thinking about," Justyn confessed. "But not for hemp; of Nic' and me."

"It's either this," Jonas commanded as if he were on Stoney. "Or a revolution soon."

"Revolution? What revolution?"

Rory turned and poked at the fire. "People are starting to wise up to the fact that they're being screwed; to see the damage being done to this world; for the sake of profit and power in the hands of just a few. Corporations, industry, consumerism is killing the entire planet."

"People are realizing how meaningless their lives are," Jonas added.

"People are evolving, Jus'. And with evolution comes revolution. Either gory or bloodless, but people are going to revolt, sooner or later."

144

Jonas turned to Justyn, "Does she know?"

"Does who know what?"

"Nicci. About you two getting married."

"Uh, no," Justyn admitted. He just now himself realized what he had said moments ago. The room was silent for some minutes before Justyn asked in general, "And what happens after the election?"

"Before the election we are going to set you up in a store to sell hemp products: Shirts, pants, jackets, paper, oil, balm, hemp butter, hemp flour, so on and so on," Rory stated. "I'll get you started. And you, Jus', you get to be CEO."

Justyn coughed up a laugh of disbelief. "I don't know anything about running a business, let alone being a CEO. Besides, I don't know if I could look in the mirror being a CEO."

"I do wish you would stop whining," Jonas sighed. "There's only going to be one store. All you'll be doing is collecting a paycheck. Besides, you're a college boy and ex-banker. What better candidate?"

"As for after the election," Rory said. "I guess that's up to you and Nicci."

"We've got plenty of time to get you up to speed," Jonas said. "We're staying 'til spring."

"That's five, six months from now," Justyn stated absently, then rose from the chair and returned to the bay window in the center of the room. Rory went to say something to Justyn, but Jonas silenced him with a glance.

Justyn stared out the window at the water in the canal. He had considered himself more of a dreamer than a doer. Yet he had never dreamt of anything like this.

So marijuana was legal here. So he likes it. So what? So what about the table and Rory's pants? Is all that reason enough to become the focal point of a controversy? But if what Rory says is true, how can he not help save the planet? After all he has said, spouted off about, bitched about. This was his chance to help fix some things. If he won, that is. He smiled. If he won.

They would have to be honest about everything. He and Nicci. Honest about their past, Justyn even thought it best to fess up to smoking marijuana here. He will have to play up the fact that he will not smoke it in the States, due to it being illegal there. Whether or not he'll actually stop if he goes back is another matter.

How will he overcome his dread of public speaking? How will he know what to say about other matters? Who is going to give him all this help? How much are they willing to pay him to do this? So many questions. He has to talk it over with Nicci. He turned to Rory, "Can we visit this factory you mentioned last night?"

"Yah, and the museum, too."

"Tomorrow?"

"We can do the factory tomorrow, the museum the day after."

Justyn returned to the leather chair and sat down. He looked up to Rory, still standing by the mantle. "I still need to think about it, discuss it with Nic'."

"Wait," Rory said and walked out of the den, leaving the door open. The cold air from the office rushed in. Jonas and Justyn sank back into their chairs, understanding the reason for the 'wings' as cold air rushed by their ankles. They heard the

door to the stairway open and Rory yell, "Wil!!?" Silence.
Then, "Is the Cat' ready for the Ijsselmeer?"

"They're home," Justyn said quietly to Jonas.

Then they heard Rory yell 'Thanks' and the door shut.

Rory began talking as he shut the door to the den
behind him. "We have a twenty-two foot open Cat in the canal
out there. You and Nicci take it and sail to the Ijsselmeer. You
can go camping on shore up the coast. There's some real nice
spots up there. I'll point them out to you on the charts."

"After the factory and museum," Justyn said, thoughts
of him and Niccole sailing alone splashing through his mind.
"That'll work. I'll be able to digest everything you're going to
show me, and then Nic' and I can talk it over."

Justyn stood and stepped over to Rory. He gestured to
shake hands. Rory took his hand without hesitation. "I really
appreciate what you and the Cap'n are trying to do," Justyn
said. "I really do. I'll give this a lot of serious thought. I'm
actually beginning to become a little interested." They released
hands and Justyn reclaimed his seat. "Now, how about lighting
that joint you're holding?"

The Ijsselmeer

The catboat was upturned on the beach of a small isle near the eastern shore on the Ijsselmeer. The Ijsselmeer, an inland lake that has been dammed off from the North Sea since the 'Thirties, was large enough that you could not see one shore from the other. A lean-to made with the sail draped over the hull hovered over Niccole and Justyn while they slept beneath it each night. During the day they would take the inflatable dinghy and explore the coastline, returning to their campsite by sunset. They had brought enough provisions to stay for another week, but they had promised Rory they would be back today. That meant leaving before noon to arrive back late tonight.

Justyn awoke before daybreak. He faced east, watching the night fade into dawn, the stars quietly disappearing into the brightening sky. Niccole was curled beneath the blankets on his bare chest, her legs draped over his. He lay there for sometime in the dark, the horizon pushing into the fresh day, Niccole warming him throughout, his thoughts sifting: *...strange things are beginning to happen...she has changed everything... the hue has changed...the tint lightened...the wind is now more a part of my breath...I feel more alive....the sun will be up soon..the first time with hope in my heart...how unique each day has become.*

The sun crept over the dawn, splashing onto them. Niccole stirred, then raised up and looked at the wink of a sun. She watched it for a moment, then turned her head and looked at Justyn. "Each sunrise is unique, you know," she whispered. "They should never be missed."

Justyn looked at the top of her head. He hadn't spoken, had he? "I understand the same is true of sunsets," he whispered back.

"Yes, it is."

They were quiet as they watched the dawn together, Niccole cuddling a little closer, chilly now that she was awake.

Moments before the sun broke free of the horizon Justyn said, "I don't want to see another sunrise or sunset without you, Nic. Ever again. Will you marry me?"

Justyn felt warm drops of moisture on his chest. "Yes," Niccole whispered. She crawled up to his face and kissed him. They made love as the day awakened.

*   *   *

"So, uh, JT. Do you have a date in mind?" Niccole was stuffing a bag with their bedding, Justyn several feet away getting the boat ready to right.

"For what?" Justyn put another half hitch around the coiled line and crammed it into a duffel bag. A small, throw pillow whizzed by his head a second later. He turned to Niccole. "Hey, that almost hit me."

Niccole shrugged. "So I missed."

"What was that for?"

"The date for us getting married, you knumbskull."

"Uh, no. I haven't thought about when." Justyn stopped what he was doing and thought a moment. "There's something that's been bothering me. Rory says he can get us both pasts that we'd be proud of. I just don't want to see you hurt."

"What are you talking about?"

Justyn looked to the ground. He didn't want to worry her. But she should know what he fears. "I'm afraid they'll go after our pasts to try to discredit us."

"Whose they?"

"The opposition. When they find out your an ex-dancer, they'll have a field day."

"I did nothing illegal. Or immoral," she demanded. Then, with sternness in her eyes, she added, "And I'm not ashamed of my past."

"Nor I," Justyn agreed. "But pushing legalization of marijuana for the campaign is an invite into our histories."

"Let 'em dig. Like I said," she crossed her arms beneath her breasts, "I got nothing to hide."

Justyn put down the rope and walked over to Niccole. He wrapped his arms around her and pulled her close. "My sentiments, exactly. Soulmate. I do want to marry you. I really don't give a shit what society thinks."

"JT!"

"Sorry, Nic. See what talking about society does to me? That's why I'm still not sure about this governor thing." He let her go and went back to the boat.

"Could've fooled me." Niccole zipped up the bedding bag and moved over to washing the dishes. "The way you've been going on and on about that museum and Rory's factory, I thought you'd decided to run."

"It's not Rory's factory. He just sends his plants there."

"I know. That's what I meant by it."

"I do think marijuana, or hemp, actually both, would help the world. And I'd like to be a part of that. But this people thing, I just don't know, Nic. I just don't know."

"I don't know either, JT. I don't know why you're making such a big thing about being in front of the public. I did it with my top off."

Justyn turned to Niccole. "That's another thing. You know that people in the public eye have no private life. Somebody could recognize you from dancing and..." He let it go, not wanting to pursue it in his mind.

Niccole turned from the wash basin to Justyn. "And, what?"

"I won't have you hurt."

"How sweet. But if I cut my hair and dress conservative, no one will ever know. Besides, the men in those clubs only looked at my tits anyway. And they were drunk."

"You can't cut that beautiful, long hair. We'll think of something else. Maybe we can dye it. Green, or blue. You know, to throw 'em off."

Niccole threw the dishrag at Justyn, missing only because he moved. Justyn retrieved the rag and tossed it back to her.

"I was only teasing."

"Just pack, Governor Thyme."

*   *   *

Thirty minutes later, Justyn flipped the boat over, then went to see if Niccole needed help.

"Maybe I'll like this governor thing and run for a second term? I understand they pay those Big Wigs pretty good. We could be set for life if we do it right. Buy a nice ketch and spend the rest of our lives sailing the oceans of the world."

"I don't know about the rest of our lives. Before I get old and gray I'd like to kick back and enjoy just being with you."

"Okay, how 'bout we find an island we can call our own? Just you and me and the pitter-patter of little feet."

"Now he wants a family."

"Not kids. Iguanas. To help with the pests in the house."

"You're such a funny man, JT."

"I'm serious. They really use 'em on the islands."

Niccole laughed, then said, "I'd love to go sailing with you, JT. You're a wonderful captain."

He shrugged. "So, we have a plan?"

"We have a plan," she said, then pulled him to her.

When they ended their embrace, Justyn said, "Um, was

that a yes?"

She tickled his ribs, "Yes. That's a yes. Knumbskull."

He gently resisted as he backed away. "Come on. Help me put the boat in the water."

Back to Amsterdam

The little catboat was on a starboard tack, her bow pointing as close to the wind as possible as they headed south on the Ijsselmeer. Niccole sat on the windward side of the cockpit going over the chart. Justyn was at the tiller, his mind on the future and the decision for Rory and Jonas.

"I can't find the canal Rory mentioned," Niccole said in mild frustration.

Justyn looked at his bride-to-be with a new found optimism. Things were going to work out. Even if he doesn't win the election, which he highly suspects will be the case, he was going to see about Rory paying him enough for his troubles so they can live at sea on a boat of their own. "Here, you take the helm and I'll see if I can find it."

"Here," she handed him the chart without rolling it back up, "I'd much rather steer than navigate, anyway."

Justyn took the crinkled chart and waited until Niccole had a hand on the tiller before switching places. The boat bumped around a few minutes before Niccole settled the cat back into its track.

As Justyn studied the chart his thoughts kept returning to the decision he had to make. Could he really make a difference? Is this the best way? Could he do it? Ah, the canal.

"Here's the canal, Nic'." He looked up from the chart to the slow moving shoreline in the distance, then back down at the chart. After a moment he asked for their heading.

"One seven zero," Niccole stated.

Justyn did the conversion from compass to True in his head and checked the chart again. He turned to Niccole, "Stay on that heading. We should see the canal in about two hours off the port bow, maybe three. "

"Have you decided yet on running for governor?"

Justyn turned back to the chart. "Not yet."

"I think you should. It's time the truth was out. Maybe this'll bring out more of them."

"More of what?"

"Truths."

"I dunno, Nicci. Sometimes I think it'll just be a waste of time and someone will end up getting hurt." He was thinking of her again. Nobody should get hurt. But politics, from what little he knew, is a harsh game. "Other times I think this may just be what the people need to open their eyes to the waste and destruction around them. Then other times I convince myself that all that'll happen is I'll get laughed at. I just don't know, Nicci." He turned and faced the bow, the wind in his face.

Niccole checked the sail, the water ahead, then looked

at Justyn. He turned back to her.

"Hey, you're suppose to be sailing. Not staring at me."

She smiled and glanced quickly ahead, then back at him. "I know what I'm doing."

"Sometimes, you know, when I think about running, I mean actually seriously think about running; when I let myself do that, I get this feeling that I should. Like it's what I'm suppose to do."

"I say go with that feeling. You'd make a grand governor."

"That's twice now."

"Twice what?"

"Twice you've elected me."

"There's nothing wrong with a little positive thinking."

"Sail the boat."

*   *   *

Rory was in the den, working at his desk. It was late evening and the desk lamp was the only light on, a cup of herb tea steaming to one side, a notebook for one of his gardens open in front of him. The dim glow from the canal lights through the window shrouded the rest of the den in a haunted hue. He saw movement outside the window out of the corner of his eye and looked towards it. The mast of his catboat slid into view. The sail was up.

"Jus' is a heck of sailor bringing that thing in under sail," he muttered to himself.

He got up and went to the window to watch the final approach. He smiled at himself when he saw Niccole at the tiller, Justyn ready to release the halyard at the right moment.

Suddenly the sail dropped and Justyn jumped from the boat with a mooring line to shore. He quickly got his feet planted and pulled the boat to a halt, the bumpers hanging over the side mushing gently. Moments later Justyn and Niccole were tying the sail to the boom.

Rory turned from the window and lit the fireplace before heading downstairs to inform the others.

Justyn and Niccole were dragging their gear up the walk, heads down and had not heard the front door open.

"Well?"

Justyn jerked his head up, startled. It was Jonas. He stood on the porch, silhouetting him in the light of the doorway.

"You've got to learn patience," Justyn said, an impressive impression of Jonas.

"Don't get wise. Did you make your decision?"

"Yes, Uncle Jonas. I did."

Jonas ignored Justyn and stepped off the porch to help Niccole.

"Well?" he asked Justyn again as he grabbed the largest bag Niccole was carrying.

"We need to talk."

One Evening Four Months Later

The sun just having set, the darkness getting an early grip. The men were in the den, endlessly prepping Justyn for his new role. Natalie was in a second floor bathroom, soaking in bubble bath while reading a book and sipping wine. Niccole and Wilhemina sat in the kitchen, chatting.

"JT's hair is getting long," Wilhemina said to Niccole. "Sure is pretty."

They were sitting at the kitchen table, the fireplace the only light, illuminated the kitchen in shadows and silhouettes that danced and swayed to independent rhythms.

Niccole had her elbows on the table, coffee cup held

high, her back arched forward as she leaned on her arms. "It'll be longer than mine by time we get back to L.A. Jonas thinks he'll need to have it cut by then, not just trimmed. I think he looks like Jesus Christ now." Niccole lowered her arms, resting the cup on the table without letting go and leaned forward, lowering the volume of her voice. "Kinda puts a new twist in our sex life." She sat back, raising the cup back to position.

Wilhemina giggled, still a little high from the joint her, Niccole and Natalie smoked after dinner.

"Let's not begin again about twists in the sex life. My gut hurt for two days after that night we talked about..twists."

Wilhemina giggled again. Niccole laughed out loud.

When she stopped laughing moments later, Niccole said, "I think I envy you."

"For what? My penis!?"

"No. Your orgasms." They both laughed.

"Let me say this," Wilhemina started, again leaning forward to Niccole. She spoke in a whisper, "Before I met Rory, I considered my penis a curse. Like it was an affliction or something. That's why I worked in a funeral home."

"Are you sure you want to tell me this, Wil? It isn't necessary."

"Ah, yah 'tis. I like you a lot and want you to know who I am."

"I like you, too, Wil. You don't need to tell me this, though. It's..it's too personal."

"I want to tell you, Nicci. Please."

Niccole nodded, slightly ashamed to be listening to something so intimate, but also touched to be considered so close.

"I was ashamed of myself for what nature had done to me: a hermaphrodite. Almost. No balls but a penis that's connected to nothing but the blood stream. All the damn thing will do is stiffen. And did I tell you I can never have children?"

Niccole shook her head, sadness for her new friend obvious in her eyes.

"I didn't think anyone would ever love me the way Rory does. Not with all that is wrong with me.

Niccole reached across the table and touched Wilhemina's hand. "There's not a thing wrong with you. You're just different and most people are scared of different."

"You know, I use to want to be normal, like everybody else. I even checked into how much it would cost to get the... the affliction removed.

"Even when I first met Rory I still wanted it gone. But we talked about it a lot and took the sex slow. We are happy with it." She leaned close to Niccole and whispered, "You don't think Rory is gay, do you? Or maybe bi?"

Niccole thought for a moment, then answered with a question. "Does it matter?"

"No. Not to me. But, I was a little concerned what other people thought."

Again, Niccole volleyed with a question, the same question. "Does it matter?"

"I certainly hope not."

"Oh. I see what you mean. Well, how many people know about your... affliction?"

"Just the ones close. Most of Rory's business acquaintances have no idea, if not all. Our family's never bring it up. Well, at least when I'm around.

"Rory was kind of slow to touch it at first, now that I think about it. It was, wow, over three months after we started having sex."

"There's your answer, you twit. He's not gay. He's just in love with you and is willing to whatever he can to make you happy."

Wilhemina sat quiet for several moments before looking into Niccole's eyes and saying, "I'm not a twit." She then smiled.

"I think we'll be friends for a long time, Wil. I got this feeling."

Wilhemina smiled, "Yah. And pretty soon I will tell my friends here that I know a governor's wife in America. Won't I be the envy?"

"You'd have better luck telling them about your affliction." They laughed again. "Besides," Niccole added, "there's a good chance he won't win."

"Good. Then you could come back sooner."

Niccole smiled. "That would be nice. But we still have some time, Jonas says we're leaving sometime next month."

"Yah. We had a mild winter this year. Spring is coming early. You will write? Let me know how you two are doing and the campaign."

"You know I will, Wil." Niccole paused, unsure of what she just said, going over it quickly in her mind. "I'll call you when we get the store setup. Maybe you'll come visit, hunh?"

Wilhemina looked towards the coffee pot, then back to Niccole. "How's your coffee? Mine needs a filling."

Niccole heard the evasiveness in Wilhemina's voice.

She had forgotten that Rory was here under sanctuary. "No. I'm fine."

As Wilhemina rose to freshen her coffee, Niccole added, "I suppose it wouldn't be much fun without Rory. I'm sorry, Wil. I wasn't thinking."

Wilhemina sat back down at the table before speaking, "Not only would it not be any fun, it could very well be dangerous."

"Now you lost me. Why would it be dangerous for you to come to L.A.?"

"You know of Denise?"

Niccole shook her head.

"Ah, 'tis a horrid story. Let me get the pot an' I'll tell ya'."

Niccole reached across the table and held Wilhemina's hand this time. "I'm sure gonna miss you until we can get back here."

"Me, too." Wilhemina twisted and rose, headed for the coffee pot on the counter.

*   *   *

"Ain't it about time for a break," Justyn said as he closed the book and placed it on the notepad on the hemp table. Jonas sat in the other wing chair, also reading. Rory was at his desk, writing in a notebook.

"What'd I tell you about whining? And it ain't ain't," Jonas said without looking from his book.

"Ain't it, Cap'n?" Justyn snipped.

"Don't get wise?!"

"It's time for a break," Rory interjected into the tensing

conversation. "Why don't you take a walk, Jus'. Ask Wil to bring up the tea tray while you're down there, too. I'll have a joint ready for you when you get back."

"I.."

"He don't need to smoke," Jonas over spoke.

Justyn glared at Jonas. He then inhaled deeply, letting it out slow as he stood and turned to Rory. "I don't think I want to. Thanks anyway."

"Go for the walk. See if Nicci would mind going with you."

"Yeah," Justyn said, then left the den.

When they heard the far door shut, Jonas spoke first.

"He really shouldn't smoke too much. I don't want him forgetting everything he's learned."

Rory smiled. He had been preaching about marijuana to Jonas since he met him. Still, he had to point details out to him. "That comes from chronic use. Abuse. And you don't forget everything." Rory giggled then, unable to suppress it any longer. "You just forget current events. Sometimes. And they're not gone forever."

"Nevertheless."

"Why don't you join us when Jus' gets back? Just for a while? When's the last time you smoked the Lady?"

"Ummm, that night after telling JT our plan."

"No wonder you're so irritable. You need to relax."

"Now don't you start in."

Early Spring Walk

Niccole and Justyn walked on the canal side of the street. The full moon was on their left, overlooking the canal from a clear sky. Niccole was nearest the water with the railing inches from her arm. Justyn had his gaze to the ground when he said, "I don't understand what's gotten into Jonas. It's almost as if he's spiteful."

"Maybe he's just been on land too long?" Niccole said and pulled Justyn closer. It was cold after the sun went down.

"You know, it's almost as if he's trying to piss me off."

"JT! You know you need to stop talking like that."

"Sorry. I thought I could be myself around you."

"What makes you think I like to hear talk like that?"

"I've heard you say worse."

"You need to relax, my love. Maybe you should ask

Rory for a joint when we get back."

"He's already offered. I told him I didn't want any."

"Why not?"

They walked several steps, turning to cross the bridge spanning the canal before Justyn replied, "You know, I can't honestly say why not. I guess because it's illegal everywhere but here. Plus, I like it. I don't want to get hooked on it or anything, you know."

"You can't really get hooked on it. It's not like it's heroin or cigarettes or alcohol."

They stopped at the crest of the bridge, elbows on the stone, looking down at the water.

"How 'bout we go back and go to bed? That'll relax me."

"Funny man. I don't want you taking your aggression out on me. After the joint with Rory. Maybe." She paused, then added absently, "I kinda like that pudgy, little guy. He's a sweetheart."

"Yeah, but he's a bitch to work for."

"JT!"

"Sorry."

"You need to realize that most people don't really care to hear that kind of talk."

"Yeah. Reminds them of how close to being barbaric we still are."

"Must you be so sarcastic?!"

"I'd change if the world would change."

"Well it's not going to, my love. And if you don't, it's going to kill you. Now come on. Let's walk some more. It's too cold to just stand here."

As they walked the quiet streets Niccole rambled on about different people she knew who smoked marijuana. Among them were six artists she knew rather well..."I use to rent my garage to a band, Glass Reality, on Saturdays so they could practice. That's how I knew them. The writer I knew from the joint I was working in at the time.

"Jonas reminded me of him because he use to come into the club just to play pool and drink citrus juice. I think he was stoned when he came in. I talked to him a little bit at the club while we shot a game or two of pool, and he eventually asked me out for coffee. Said he wanted to get my life story down. Thought he might use me in a story sometime, maybe even the one he was currently working on. He was cute and he also bought breakfast. And all he wanted was my story. That's what was really sweet about it.

"He was the stoner of the bunch. The musicians were potheads. Hard core potheads, but still pot-heads. Sebastion, though, was a stoner."

"Stoner, pothead, what's the difference?"

"Potheads smoke to relax or do something artistic, creative. Like Glass Reality. They'd get to the garage straight and start smoking as soon as they unloaded the car.

"Sebastion smoked from the time he woke up 'til he crashed. And that could be four hours later, or forty-four. For him that, was normal. With or without the weed. Ever since his writing made him enough money so he didn't have to work a steady job, he'd been on his own schedule."

"Sebastion?"

"Sebastion Bucansin."

Justyn thought a moment. "I've heard of him. Never

read any of his books, but I have heard of him."

"I bet we can find him in a book shop here."

"We'll look tomorrow."

"Sounds good. We'll see if we can find, Solitaire."

"That one of his?"

Niccole nodded. "A short story collection. Pretty good."

"How long did you know him?"

"About a year. Before he was killed."

"Oh. Wow. I'm sorry. Killed? How?"

"Oh geez. It's a long story."

"Just give me the condensed version."

She stopped by a bench in front of a coffee shop.

Justyn looked in the window and saw the menu for their selection of coffee, pastries, and marijuana. "Wanna' go in?"

"For?"

"I dunno. The way you whined about it being a long story I thought a good joint and some strong coffee might help ease the telling and warm our insides."

She looked to the window, at her reflection, amazed how long ago it had been since Sebastion's death. "Yeah, let's go in. A joint sounds good. So does coffee." As he stepped in front of her to open the door, she reached forward and pinched his butt.

"Ow. What the hell?"

"I didn't whine."

They sat next to the window they had just been staring in, waiting for the marijuana to arrive as they sipped at the steaming, French Roast coffee. The table was round and small.

A cup held books of matches. Another sugar and cream packets and a small, glass vase with a single flower left little room for coffee cups, much less elbows. There was no tablecloth covering the dark wood.

"So," Justyn said after a sip of coffee, "how did this writer die?"

"One of his ex-girlfriend thought a character in one of his books was about her. She didn't like what he did to her in the story so, she did some research on the Internet and found his address. Then she drove halfway across the country to shoot him when he answered the door."

The waitress arrived with the marijuana, placing the little, chromed tray with the two joints close to Justyn. Niccole reached over and selected one, picking up a book of matches as she retracted her arm. Justyn paid and tipped the waitress while Niccole fired up the marijuana cigarette. "You gonna share that or do we both get one?"

"Share. We'll take the other one home." She handed him the joint.

He held his fingers against the back of hers for a moment, staring deep into her eyes. He could see this was troubling for her.

"I'm fine," she said, reading his eyes. "I just haven't thought about this for a long time. It's been over five years."

"Know what she was on?"

"Know what who was on?" Justyn looked to the waitress.

"Not her, the woman that shot Sebastion."

Justyn shook his head, passing the joint back to her.

"Anti-depressants. Killed herself two months later

waiting for her trial. Sad thing was, her death made bigger news than his." She inhaled from the joint, then passed it to Justyn.

It was getting short. Justyn was fiddling with it, trying to hold it without burning his fingers when the waitress arrived with a small alligator clip dressed up with a couple of beads and a feather. It was now a roach clip.

"Thanks," Justyn told the waitress as she handed it to him. She nodded, turned, and walked away.

"It's a real shame too," Niccole rambled on. "He was quite a guy. Really different. He didn't belong anywhere. Everywhere I saw him he didn't fit in. Even in the strip club, he stuck out like a sore thumb. I guess when he told me he smoked so much weed because he is on the outside of society looking in, I guess he was right. He said he needed the drugs to stay sane.

"But as long as he was smoking weed he was pretty much happy-go-lucky and easy-going. But if he was off of it for a few days, specially if it wasn't his idea, he was moody and quick tempered. Like most artists.

"Maybe that's what I need to do."

"What?"

"Become a stoner."

"We'd have to live here."

Justyn looked out the window for a few moments before turning back to Niccole. He shrugged. "No big deal. I'd work for Rory in one of his gardens. Be his quality control. We could save up for a boat and in a few years sail away."

She looked at him with warmth and smiled. "Well, JT. I do declare: The dreamer has returned."

Justyn smiled, knowing it was because of her that his hopes have returned. His allowance of himself to dream again was because of her. His happiness, near euphoria, was because of her. Albeit, right now the marijuana was helping the euphoric feeling. "So, what happened to the musicians?" He finally got the joint in the roach clip without crushing the joint. He lit it and inhaled, then passed the roach clip to Niccole.

"Glass Reality?"

Justyn nodded.

"They hit the road. Far as I know they're still touring."

Dialogue with the Lady

"Where's the Cap'n?" Justyn said as he sat in the leather chair on the window side. Rory sat in the other on his right, steadying a cup of tea on the arm of the chair. The serving tray sat on the table. The fireplace the only source of internal light, the heat from it warming Justyn's still chilly frame.

"You took too long on your walk. He went to bed. How was your walk by the way?"

"Cold. Otherwise nice. Stopped at a coffee shop on the other side of the canal and had a few cups and a joint." Justyn reached into his shirt pocket and pulled out a joint. "Brought one home."

"No wonder you were gone so long." Rory took a sip of tea. "There's another cup there. Make yourself some tea. We'll light that joint afterwards." He sipped at the tea again, then balanced it on the right arm of the chair, his fingers touching the rim of the saucer. "Which shop did you say? Right across the canal by the Molukkenstraat bridge?"

"That's easy for you to say. You should be able to see it from the window."

"Really. If that's the case, the joint you brought home I sold to them. Let me see it."

Justyn leaned forward and handed Rory the joint, then tilted towards the table and selected a tea. He sat back as it steeped, "I don't know if I should smoke anymore, Rory."

"Why not?" Rory ran the marijuana cigarette under his nose and inhaled.

"I'm pretty stoned as it is. I don't want to OD."

Rory suppressed all but a chuckle. "Can't OD. You can pass out. But you can't OD."

"I doubt I'll get any stoner. More stoned?"

Rory handed the joint back. "It's Northern Lights. Here. You and Nicci smoke it together." Justyn took the joint and put it back in the pocket he pulled it out from. "And you most likely could get stoner." Justyn started to pull the joint back out when Rory stopped him, "No no no. You keep that. Do with it like I said. You and Nicci.

"I'll go get one that'll get you stoner." He let go of the saucer and the tea balanced on the arm of the chair without his help.

Justyn sighed. The desk lamp clicked on then,

throwing a brighter glow on the mantle.

"Darn. Where'd I put the case," Rory said to himself. "I just filled it."

Justyn stared at the fire, listening to Rory mumbling to himself while rustling through drawers and pigeon holes. Then Rory started humming, the search continuing. Suddenly there was silence, the crackling fire and gusty winds whispering confidence to Justyn.

"Here it is," Rory announced. A moment later he sat on the edge of the chair. "It's a blend."

"A blend? Of what?" Justyn adjusted his position and reached for his tea and saucer. He sat back in a fluid motion, setting the saucer on his thighs.

"Northern-Lights, Skunk, uh, a bunch more."

Justyn noticed something different about Rory, but couldn't really pin down what it was; there was something about his voice, about his look, about his mannerisms. But Justyn couldn't say what it was. Then an idea darted into his mind. "How much have you smoked tonight, Rory?"

"This'll make three. Four? Three."

"Are you sure you need anymore?"

"Oh I'm fine," he waved Justyn off. "Just haven't been this high in a while. Since before you came. All this political talk gets to me after a while." Rory grabbed a match before sitting back into the plush of the chair. It crunched and squeaked as it pulled his form in. He struck the match with his thumbnail and lit the joint, inhaling slow and deep. He handed it to Justyn.

Justyn took the joint from Rory's fingers and inhaled deeply. They passed it back and forth for several more minutes before Rory laid his arm on the arm of the chair, the joint idling between his fingers.

Justyn raised the cup to his lips and blew gently across the top. When he felt it was enough, he tipped the cup to his mouth and sipped tenderly. He set it back in the saucer on his lap. "You don't really think I have any chance, do you?"

"For governor? No. But I like to dream."

"So, why are we doing it?"

"There are already have several states with medicinal marijuana laws and laxed possession laws. It's time we turn it all the way around and get everyone growing it so we can stop using fucking oil! You, my friend, are the States wake up call.

"That deal in Canada I told you about before?"

"The H2K one?"

Rory nodded. "It's been running eighteen wheelers back and forth across the country on H2K for the past seven months. We started it up just before you got here last fall."

"We? I thought you just held an interest?"

"Okay. A big interest. Basically, it's my company, but I have partners."

"I guess it's no longer a secret then?"

"Never was a secret. The oil companies are scrambling to shut us down. But, by this time next year, we will have shut out the oil companies from Canada."

"Just how rich are you? If you don't mind me asking?"

"Not very. My partners in H2K have lots more money than me. I just had this idea of making H2K. They liked the idea, but they wanted silent partnerships because of the trouble with the oil companies that it could bring."

Justyn watched the fire burn for a minute, again unsure

what to do, then asked, "Is there enough left for me to get a hit?"

"Actually, no. This one needs a crutch. However," Rory handed Justyn a fresh joint. "I rolled more than one of these."

Justyn took the joint and drew it under his nose, smelling the aroma of the flower inside. He reached to the table and grabbed a match, sitting back heavily. "Where's the footstool?" he asked Rory.

Rory stood with a groan, "I used it to reach a book earlier today." He poked at the fire before disappearing into the darkness behind the chairs.

Justyn tried to stop him, but Rory hushed him with a sideways glance.

Rory strolled back into the loom of the fireplace on Justyn's side as Justyn struck the match. Justyn jerked when Rory caught his eye, the match nearly going out.

"Pardon me, Jus'. I didn't mean to startle you."

"Hunh? No. Uh, nevermind." Justyn lifted his feet as Rory put the covered footstool beneath them.

"Thanks. Must be that walk. My legs feel stiff. I'll have to go for another walk tomorrow." He put the joint in his mouth and lit it.

"Perhaps I'll go with you; if you don't mind? I could use the exercise myself. Wonder if I can talk that ol' salt into walking with us?" Rory said the last sentence to himself, picking a match from the shot glass before sitting down.

"Not if he's gonna be irritable."

"Ah. He just misses his boat and the water. Don't let him get to you."

"Maybe he should go to the Ijsselmeer?"

"Jonas sail something besides Stoney? Not until she sinks."

Rory lit the match, then the remainder of his joint. He tossed the lit match into the fireplace. It burned with ferocity for several seconds then crumbled to the embers below.

Justyn inhaled deeply from his joint. Exhaling, he queried, "So, if your company in Canada is going to bring you trouble, what kind of trouble should I be expecting?"

"There won't be an attempt on your life or anything like that. You won't be that big of a threat. But I suspect there will be demonstrations, unkind media coverage and a lot of name calling. The usual political bullshit."

"Just as long as nobody hurts Nicci. They can say what they want about me, but I won't have anyone bothering her."

"Just keep your cool. I'm sure somebody will say something about her background."

"I'm sure of that too. But they can be nice about it." He drew in from the joint, holding the smoke as long as he could. "I just don't want her hurt."

"I would hate for that to happen, Jus'."

Time floated as they smoked in the quiet crackling of the fire.

Wedding at Sea

It was late morning, near the end of April, puffy clouds sailing across the sky as Rory and Wilhemina waved from the docks while StoneAge Wizard motored away. Jonas was at the helm, Niccole on the forepeak as lookout. Natalie and Justyn stood at the transom, waving. StoneAge Wizard had been in the Netherlands over five months. She was leaving with a fresh caulking on her hull and three new coats of varnish. New sails hung from her masts.

When they had motored some distance from the dock, their friends on shore but tiny silhouettes, the wind hit them on the starboard side with a gust. Justyn turned to go forward and raise the mainsail when Jonas bellowed, "Hoist the sails!"

*   *   *

The sail down the coast to the Canary Islands was quick. They were all kept busy during their watches due to heavier shipping traffic and then high seas. They were all grateful when they reached the Canary's, even Jonas. They stayed for five days hunkered down in a sheltered harbor, waiting out a storm.

The sea was quieter south of the Canary's and down Western Africa. The sun was out most days and clear nights meant for easier navigation. They were able to relax and enjoy the sail. Justyn started reading the books that Rory had sent along. Niccole and Jonas talked about the shop that her and Justyn were to run. Natalie improved at the helm.

On around the Cape of Good Hope and into the Indian Ocean the weather remained sunny and breezy. It also gave time enough for Justyn to approach Jonas one sunny and hot afternoon while in the Indian Ocean.

"Wha'd'ya doing up so early, JT?" Jonas asked when Justyn sat down in the cockpit across from him. "This is really some scary reading," he said, putting the book on Machiavelli down. "What's up? Besides you."

"I was wondering. Uh, we were wondering."

Jonas raised a brow.

"Since you're the captain of Stoney..well..uh..would you marry Nicci and me?"

"Nicci and I."

"No, Nic and me. You have Nat'."

Jonas was unimpressed with the humor. "I'd be happy to. But what about somebody recognizing her and causing trouble? There's still that possibility."

Justyn turned to the companionway, "NICCI!" A moment later, a young woman with caramel skin, green lucent eyes and a pixie haircut appeared in the opening.

Jonas almost didn't recognize her. The haircut had done wonders. "I don't believe it," Jonas said, surprised. He turned to Justyn as Niccole stepped on deck, "She really looks different."

Justyn sat with a silly smirk. "I know. And wearing conservative clothes and fake glasses, it'll be almost impossible to recognize her."

Niccole sat by Justyn, sliding her arm behind him. He put his right hand on her knee.

"You look gorgeous. Ten years younger," Jonas said.

"Nat' said five," Niccole paused as she turned from Jonas to Justyn and back. "JT still has to get used to it."

"She had long hair back in junior high."

"Would you believe this fool put it in a plastic bag and put it away."

Jonas nodded, then nodded towards Justyn. "This fool is madly in love with you. And this fool," he touched the brim of his hat with a slight nod, "would be honored to marry you two. NAT!?"

Niccole rocked forward and placed her hand on Jonas' knee. "She knows."

"Figures," Jonas said with a sigh. "When?"

"Tomorrow morning? At dawn. If it's not too early for you two?"

"How long have you two been discussing this?"

Niccole and Justyn looked at each other, then turned to Jonas. Justyn then said, "Since Ijsselmeer."

"How long has Nat' known?"

"I told her the day we left," confessed Niccole.

"Figures," Jonas sighed.

*   *   *

The next morning, as the glow from the sun brightened the eastern sky from below the horizon, Stoneage Wizard was headed into the glow on autopilot. The jib and staysail were furled tight, wrapped with coloured line. The main and foresail were reefed for storm, tacked on a close reach. StoneAge Wizard glided through the water on a slight heel unattended as a ceremony of man began. The swells were shallow and spaced. It made for a gentle ride.

The captain and crew were on the foredeck, the bride and groom facing forward, the inner stay between them. With his shoulder against the forestay, Jonas faced the stern of the boat. Natalie, the bride's maid, stood off to port, steadying herself with a stanchion. King Neptune was Justyn's best man off starboard.

Justyn was wearing his best shirt, a bold Hawaiian floral print Niccole bought for him in the Caribbean. His hair was in a tight pony-tail, tied once close to his head and again below his shoulders. The pants were a gift from Rory: blue jeans made from hemp. His feet were bare.

Niccole wore the wedding dress Wilhemina had given to her. She didn't wear the veil nor train, but was still a beautiful bride. She did have to take the dress in around the waist and bust, but it clung to her frame with a sensual dignity. Her short hair accentuated the lines of her face, her eyes glowing in the loom of sunrise.

The ceremony was similar to a marriage on terra firma, except more of Jonas' words were of nature and the love of it. Here, where the wind filled your sails and the sea was your bed, the words seemed fitting.

And Jonas had timed it perfectly, for when the sun peeked over the edge of the earth, he ended his monologue with, "You may now kiss the bride."

As Justyn and Niccole embraced, Jonas quietly turned around and removed the leather pouch hanging from his neck, Natalie watching intently. He held the pouch over the bow wave for several heartbeats, then let the string slip through his fingers. "Bye, Mom," he whispered.

Natalie stepped over to him and put an arm around his waist, drawing herself close. He looked down at her and shrugged. "Feels right," he said.

She nodded, then left.

Jonas, staring out to sea, remembered...

...They had been fighting a storm in the Indian Ocean for thirty-six hours when the accident happened. Jonas had been helping on deck since the start, over his mother's protest. She argued that it was too dangerous for a fifteen year-old boy. His father had insisted, demanding that Jonas help. He had said that Jonas needed to know the sea and, he needed the help.

It was when young Jonas was at the helm that his father was killed, early in the evening of the second day of the storm. Father had gone forward to reef the mainsail again.

Jonas watched with a knot in his stomach as his father wrestled with the sail in the heavy seas. When he started back twenty minutes later Jonas breathed a sigh of relief. Then the boat was hit by a rogue wave.

StoneAge Wizard lurched and rolled hard. Jonas watched in astonished horror as the mainmast boom broke loose the vang and swung across the boat, striking his father on the side of the head and knocking him into the water. Jonas, his body shaking uncontrollably, watched his father float by before he could find his voice and call to his mother. Jonas then tossed the lifering over the side He had to turn around and go back

When his mother reached him moments later, Jonas quickly explained what had happened. The fear in her eyes caused him to stop shaking. He had to take care of things. Jonas told his mother to start the engine then left the cockpit to tie down the loose boom.

After securing the boom, Jonas checked where his father's head had hit. He found blood, too much blood. He also found clumps of hair, skin, and chunks of bone. His father was dead before he hit the water. Jonas was sure of that. His father was dead.

Upon returning to the cockpit Jonas told his mother of his findings. She went hysterical. After getting his mother below and into some dry clothes, he put her in the starboard bunk. He raised and secured the webbing to keep her from rolling out, then leaned over the top of the webbing and said, "Don't worry, Mother. I'll get us through this. You'll be safe here."

Back at the helm he released the bungee cord and turned away from the wind. There was enough fuel for seven hours of running. Jonas looked to the sky. The sun would be back up in six. If he hadn't found his father by dawn, he would end the search and get his mother to the closest port - Cocos Island, if he remembered the charts correctly.

Dawn arrived and Justyn didn't find his father. "Looks like you feed the fish one last time, Cap'n," he said to the sea. He bungeed the helm and went forward to raise the sails to a heavy weather reef. Back in the cockpit, he turned off the engine and sailed StoneAge Wizard for four more days before reaching land. He checked on his mother from time to time, but the boat kept him pretty much occupied.

It was early morning on the third day that she came on deck. "How can you just keep sailing? I think I can understand the storm forcing you to, but that was over yesterday. How can you just turn off your emotions like that? Didn't you love your father?"

Jonas glared at his mother, tears in his eyes. "I loved the Cap'n with all my heart, Mother." Jonas pounded his chest with his fist, "With all my heart!" He put both hands back on the wheel and watched the sea. "I had to keep sailing or the storm would have killed us, too."

"Maybe you should have let it." .

Jonas kept his gaze forward. Maybe it should have, but it didn't. It only killed father. She was all he had now. Her and Stoney. And he wasn't going to let anything happen to either one. After a moment he said, "Could you fix me a cup of soup, Mother? I'm awfully hungry."

Jonas' mother looked at her son, now a man. "Aye, Little Cap'n. Aye. Would you like a sandwich, too?"

"Aye, Mom. Aye."

When his mother died two years later, he heard her words as he put a leather pouch, a palmful of her ashes inside, around his neck: "How can you just turn off your emotions..?" Then he rowed the dinghy to Stoney and sailed away.

Pitcairn

They were in the middle of the South Pacific, anchored at St. Paul's Point on Pitcairn. Up the north-east coast of the island is Bounty Bay, where the H.M.S. Bounty was lost in a fire.

They were just ending a week of rest before going on to the Galapagos; Jonas' wedding present to Niccole and Justyn. They expected to be back in Los Angeles in eight to twelve weeks.

Niccole and Justyn had taken the tender south, spear fishing for dinner and a few days beyond. Natalie and Jonas stayed with StoneAge Wizard to prep her for an early departure. The task completed, they sat across from each other in the cockpit with their feet up on the opposite seat, their legs against the others. Natalie was fiddling with his shirt with her toes. He ignored it while he watched the horizon for the tenders sail.

They sat in silence for some minutes, rocking softly on the ocean swells, StoneAge Wizard tugging gently on her anchor rodes. Jonas looked up to the sky, habit now for him, checking the weather, and the time by the sun. He looked back down at Natalie, her auburn hair glinting in the afternoon rays. It was time.

"Nat'?"

"Hmph?"

"How much do you love me?" The apprehension was blatant.

"Enough to come sailing with you. Why?" When he didn't answer right away, she got her toes under his shirt and poked him. "Why did you ask me that?"

There was a worried hue in her voice that put him straight to his point. He put his feet down, sat up straight at the edge of the seat, took a deep breath, then stumbled out, "Natalie, will you marry this ol' salt?"

Natalie sat there, dumbfounded. Her mouth hung slightly ajar, her eyes glazing over as she stared into his. "Us? Are you serious?" she stumbled out.

Relief flowed from both of them. Natalie put her feet down and sat straight.

"Yep. Which would make you, Mrs. Serious."

Natalie leaped to him, pushing him back onto the seat. StoneAge Wizard dipped, yanking at her lines. Natalie straddled Jonas, lowering her face to his. "I'll marry you anytime, anywhere," she said before suffocating him with kisses. She sat up to undo his pants.

*   *   *

Jonas laid on his back on the seat in the cockpit, Natalie sprawled out on top of him, still asleep. The sun was setting, shooting shadows of the clouds across the sky. There was about an hour of daylight left. He had been watching the sky change, the clouds streaked with colours and glistening strands of ice dancing slowly in hues. They had fallen asleep after their love making. A shift in the wind had awoken him some minutes ago.

He lay there beneath her, breathing in her scent, feeling her form on him, the steady rise and fall of her chest in sync with his, the beat of her heart on his belly. He didn't want to wake her, but he knew Justyn and Niccole would be returning soon. She felt so good there, though. Even asleep, she felt comforting. He shook her shoulder as he whispered her name, "Nat - a - lie-e-e", coaxing her from her sleep.

When she stirred, he said, "Come on, Mrs. Castle. We need to get dressed before they get back."

"Oh, you would," she groaned.

"Come on. Let's hope they caught something for dinner. I'm starved."

"Yeah, sex'll do that to ya'."

He kissed her on the forehead. "Come on, before we start up again." He moved to rise.

She grabbed his face with her hands and kissed him

hard and long on the mouth. "Oh, all right," she said when their lips parted, then climbed off him and began fastening her clothes. Jonas buttoned his pants before sitting up, leaving his shirt open.

"You want to tell them?" he asked, watching her tie her blouse beneath her breasts.

"How could I not?"

Jonas smiled. "Come on. I'll help you in the galley."

As they headed below, Jonas looked in the direction Justyn and Niccole would be coming. "There's their sail on the horizon." He looked up to his mast and checked the wind direction and speed. "They should be here in half an hour."

Below, Natalie voiced her doubts about Justyn. "So you really believe that he won't back out of this governor thing when we get back?"

"Nope. He truly believes in it," Jonas turned from the the stove to Natalie at the sink, "Rory's got him all revved up and raring to go. You've seen him reading, studying. He thinks he can make a difference. Change things.

"You should have come upstairs more often."

"If you and Rory believe in him, I guess I can too."

"The only sad thing is, he thinks he has a chance to win," he said with a tone of disbelief. "I don't understand his naiveté, but it would be some sort of miracle for him to win. Don't get me wrong, I hope he wins. I just don't see him having a chance in hell of even being in the running."

"He has the soul of a child," Natalie answered. "His heart never let go of the wonderment a child has for a puppy."

"That's because of Niccole," Jonas said. "Listening to him back at Neptune's I knew he had it in him. And after he and Nicci were together awhile, I noticed a change in him. She's opened him up."

"I hope he stays open. Men seem to have this ability to just shut off their emotions," Natalie said with frustration.

Jonas flinched, his mothers words from long ago echoing in his thoughts. He knew the reasons, and how, to shut off one's emotions, but also knew he couldn't explain it. He shrugged his shoulders. "I'm going to see if they caught anything. I'll be right back."

"I'll be left back," Natalie volleyed.

Jonas flashed a quick smile, grabbed the binoculars and went on deck, his mind elsewhere. He made his way to the foredeck and looked towards the small sail off the starboard bow. He blinked through the binoculars and spotted the tender. Justyn was looking through a telescope back at him, waving. Jonas waved back, then watched as Justyn put his monocular down and picked up a bundle of fish, raising them high so Jonas was sure to see.

Jonas waved to him again, then went back below. "They caught something to eat," he said as he climbed down the ladder. "Looks like enough for a couple nights."

"Wonder what they caught?"

He came up from behind and put his arms around her waist, giving her a gentle but firm hug. "Fish. But we'll know what kind in about twenty minutes."

Natalie turned and tapped Jonas on his shoulder.

"Ow."

"Are we still leaving in the morning?"

"I told Justyn to weigh anchor when the sky brightened. Next stop, the Galapagos. Then, Long Beach."

"How long will that give before JT starts campaigning?" Natalie asked.

"About six, eight months. In the mean time, they have a store to set up and run."

"And a wedding to attend."

Justyn Thyme, the Hemp Messiah for Governor

They found a building for their store in Santa Monica; a block away from the promenade.

The corner store that was the "Hemp Outlet" was part of a larger building that ran from the street corner to both alleys. Two stores were on either side of the Hemp Outlet; a video store and sandwich shop on the left; a liquor store and a small restaurant on the right, with parking in back. Above the stores was an apartment that ran the entire length of the building.

Justyn and Niccole stayed in that apartment. They spent most of their evenings sitting on top the roof watching the days melt into nights. The sunsets over the Pacific spectacular, each unique.

Jonas and Natalie stayed aboard StoneAge Wizard, having taken her to Marina Del Rey after the property was purchased, bringing them closer to the store. They were married a week before the store held its Grand Opening. The wedding was held onboard a charter boat halfway between California and Santa Catalina island. The captain of the charter boat did the honors.

Before the campaign for the governor began, Justyn had to campaign for the Green Party. Even with Rory's influence, there were a number of key members he had to sway to get the party backing.

The ideas Justyn spoke of at the Green Party meetings and seminars were bold, radical, and controversial. Ideas like legalizing marijuana; replacing fossil fuels with biomass, solar and wind energy; replacing synthetics products with natural ones. Ideas that sounded wonderful, as long as you weren't in the industry targeted for replacement.

He proposed how the hemp plant could help alleviate a lot of problems. The Oil Wars could be put to an end, although they'd just make up some other excuse. Hunger could be virtually eliminated. Economic salvation anywhere you could grow hemp, which is just about anywhere.

It was on these issues that Justyn Thyme was elected as the Green Party candidate to run in the next Gubernatorial race, which was four months away. He would need to start campaigning, hard.

The Powers That Be

Five months later, in a large corner office, top floor.
All the outer walls made of glass. Downtown Los Angeles
splayed out below them. They looked down on all the other
buildings and on clear days, you can see the ocean. But this
wasn't a clear day, the brown-grey haze hovered two floors
down. The pollution hung thick and stung your eyes on the
streets. In the near distance was Culver City, then the airport,
then the Pacific. A man stood at a window, looking west. He
was bald on the top of his head, the hair around the sides grey
and short - crewcut short. Late forties, maybe early fifties, but
still fit. He wore gloss black shoes, black slacks, white shirt, no

tie and a black, leather jacket. He was watching an airliner pass overhead, on its way to the airport. "Can you imagine standing here," he said, facing the window, "watching a fucking plane headed straight for you?"

"You're demented."

"And if it wasn't for my dementia," he said, still facing the window, "we wouldn't be where we are today. Your boss knows that." He turned from the window and approached the table. There were twelve of them, representatives from the oil, pharmaceutical, and paper industries, and four from the Federal Government. The man at the window was a contractor.

"This Green Party candidate is a threat. He jumped six points today, gentlemen. Six. That means people are starting to pay attention to him and the race is less than eight weeks old. We have to put a stop to him before this spreads. Before he becomes too popular and we have to wait for an opportunity, instead of now, when we can create our own."

The others shook their heads. Somebody muttered, "Not again."

"Yes. Again," the contractor stated. "And each and every time it's necessary."

"Our smear campaign will put an end to this," came a voice from down the table.

"I don't think so," said an older man across the table. He had twenty years on the contractor, less hair but longer, and several more pounds. "He's been shooting holes into every issue we bring up. We look like liars and racists."

"We are," somebody muttered.

"That's enough," came a stern warning.

"Give it some more time. Our smear campaign will

bring him down."

"So far your smear campaign has only given him more support. If we wait it'll be too late. We have to strike now. The sooner the better," this, from an Under-Secretary.

In the tense silence that followed, the contractor glanced at each attendee, reading their resolve in an instant. "I understand the problem, Mr. Under-Secretary. Your problem will go away very soon."

"Not another plane crash? Those are so complicated and convoluted, no wonder there's questions," whined the representative from the drug companies.

"Not an accident," the contractor coldly stated. "An outright assassination."

"Pretty blatant, isn't it?" complained the Under-Secretary.

"It'll be blamed on white supremacists."

They all whispered and murmured amongst themselves as the contractor lit a cigarette. "So, is the matter settled then?" he asked as he exhaled.

"Yes. Take care of this, Mr. Glanniser," the Senator stated, as if he was having his dry-cleaning sent out.

"Wait."

Mr. Glanniser tilted his head. "Mr. Under-Secretary?"

"Can it be traced back to any of us?"

"No, sir," Mr. Glanniser lied.

"Then do it; kill the pot-smoking, nigger-loving, freak," spouted the oil representative from Texas. "It'll send a message to that queer hippie across the Pond, too."

The Heckler

In one of Culver City's finest restaurants, Justyn was attending a luncheon. He was the guest speaker.

At the end of his speech, he asked for questions.

"I have one," came a man's voice from the back.

"Would you stand so I can hear you?" Justyn's voice filled the room with an electronic twang.

A man in a dark suit, white shirt and black tie, stood. His hair was cut business short and he was clean shaven. "You just want to legalize it so you can smoke it. Isn't that right?"

Justyn leaned toward the microphone, "If I wanted to smoke it, I could. Legally in several countries around the globe."

"But it was made illegal because the high is a detriment to society."

"Oil is a detriment to society," Justyn interrupted. "Oil is the major pollutant today; from our cars and trucks to plastic bottles and bags.

"The high from marijuana is often beneficial to those with a creative nature.

In fact, there's a company up in Canada that has just recently started selling H2K, a hemp-based biodiesel fuel. And now a trucking company there is using it from one coast of Canada to the other.

"Besides, the high from marijuana is no more detrimental than getting drunk. In fact, it's less damaging than alcohol.

"But that doesn't mean there shouldn't be laws regarding it's use. I would imagine those laws to be similar to laws concerning alcohol use.

"But the issue isn't the high. The issue is all the uses this annually renewable resource can be used for and the industries that are blocking it's use." Justyn leaned forward on the podium, his lips brushing the microphone. "Do you understand the concept of annually renewable resource, sir?" He paused for dramatic effect while the audience murmured. "It means fresh, raw materials every year. Every year."

"What makes these hemp products," the man in the dark suit laced 'hemp products' with spite, "any better than what we're using now?"

"Mainly, most are biodegradable, something petroleum isn't. Second, it's renewable, annually. Again, oil is a finite resource. It will run out."

"If hemp is such a wonderful, save the world plant, why aren't there any studies backing up your claims?"

Justyn leaned to the right, out of the glare and peered into the audience, searching for a face to the voice. Who does he work for?

"There have been some studies done and look promising, but the reports are suppressed. They rarely hit mainstream media. It also hasn't been too widely studied because it has been labeled a Class One narcotic. Right next to heroin and morphine.

"Besides, hemp used for industrial purposes is grown close together, so the plant grows thin and tall. It's almost all stalk. And it's the stalk and seeds we're using, not the bud. Although the flower is what gets you high, and has been used throughout the ages for its medicinal properties.

"Industrial hemp is easily recognized as what it is: an industrial crop. It has less than one percent THC in the entire plant. You could smoke an acre of it and not get a buzz.

"In any case, the high isn't dangerous. No more, even less than, alcohol. Nor is it detrimental when smoked wisely.

"Doesn't it strike you as odd that one is allowed but the other is not?"

"No, it doesn't seem odd," came the voice from the back. "It's an illegal substance and it's dangerous."

"It is not dangerous. Many creative minds use it. Hallucinogenic drugs can be enlightening, when used properly. That's were education comes in..."

The man in the dark suit turned to leave, stopping at the door. "There are those who think you're just an arrogant pothead and that you should be stopped," he shouted, then scurried through the doorway.

When the door clicked shut, Justyn asked, "Uh, anymore questions?"

"Mr. Thyme?" a woman's voice came from Justyn's left, up front and close.

Justyn turned his head to the voice.

"Yes? And please, call me, JT."

"JT," the reporter paused, feeling a little odd referring to the candidate by his nickname, "Mr. Thyme, what about legalizing other narcotics?"

"My team and I have been studying programs done in the Netherlands and Canada on weaning addicts off of heroin."

"Mr. Thyme?"

"Mr. Thyme?"

"Mr. Thyme?"

"JT?"

Rudy

Justyn was on his way home from StoneAge Wizard, having gone there after the luncheon. The idea of the heckler threatening him had Justyn a little concerned. Would somebody actually cause trouble? He and Jonas, after a lengthy debate, resolved to call Rory in the morning.

The cab dropped Justyn off in front of the restaurant next to the store. He went inside and made a reservation with Rudy, the maitre'de. He then walked up to the Hemp Outlet, catching Natalie as she came out the front door.

"Meet you on the Promenade later? You and Jonas,"

Justyn confirmed. "I'll buy ya' guys an ice cream cone, to share."

"Only if Nicci puts the leash on you."

"Around eight?"

"See ya' then."

Justyn gave Natalie a peck on the cheek. She slapped him on the shoulder, giggling as she walked away.

Justyn closed the door behind him and stood at the entrance as he looked for Niccole. Spotting her at the counter, he yelled from the door, "Is it closing time?"

"Past. Lock up."

Justyn locked the doors and pulled down the shades. He walked over to Niccole and hugged her from behind.

"How 'bout we scoot down to Rudy's for dinner?"

"It's Valentine's. Rudy's just a host."

"Maitre'de."

"Whatever." She turned in his arms and faced him. "Is he working tonight?"

"Yep. Made reservations."

"Help me finish closing."

*   *   *

Half an hour later Justyn and Niccole sat at their table in Valentine's, chatting as they waited for their food. The crowd was moderate and the room relatively quiet. Justyn and Niccole spoke at sedated levels.

"How was business today? Did it pick up after lunch?"

"A little. How was your speech?"

"Not bad. Did have a heckler at the end; during the Q

201

and A part. The little shit threatened me."

"Threatened? How? Who?"

Justyn shrugged. "The heckler said I should be stopped. Called me a pothead."

She reached across the table and touched his hand. "You're not a pothead. You hardly smoke."

"I know, but they don't."

"Who did he work for?"

"I dunno. Could be about anybody. What we're doing is going to affect a lot of people, a lot of different industries. I just wonder what they wanted."

"Probably to see if you're as cute as everybody says you are."

Justyn smiled. "Right."

"You worry too much."

"Probably."

Rudy arrived with a bottle of wine. Justyn looked at the bottle presented to him, then to Rudy.

"We didn't order any wine, Rudy."

"Compliments of the house, Mr. Thyme. For the polls."

"The polls?" Justyn said as he turned to Niccole.

Niccole shrugged, "Haven't seen 'em."

"You are in third, Mr. Thyme. The wine should go well with your meal."

Justyn looked at the wine again. It was white. He nodded at Rudy, "You know there's only three of us running."

Rudy nodded with a smile. "But before you weren't even listed. Now, people are starting to listen to Mr. JT."

Justyn looked at Niccole. "I'm on the polls."

Niccole shrugged. "Told you you were cute."

"Come back after closing and we'll smoke a doobie," Rudy said in a whisper. "My treat."

"We'll try to get back here by nine-thirty," Justyn said. "We might be bringing some friends, if that's okay?"

Rudy turned to Justyn, "I only have the one joint. I.."

Justyn hushed him by raising a hand. "I'll pick some up on the Promenade. We can go to the apartment."

"That would be grand."

"Good. We'll see you at nine-thirty." Justyn took the bottle of wine from Rudy's hands.

Rudy handed Justyn a corkscrew, "Ten."

After Rudy left, Niccole kicked Justyn in the leg.

"Ow!"

"What do you think you're doing?"

"That hurt, ya' know."

"Good. It was suppose to hurt. How would it look if a candidate for governor is arrested for buying pot on the streets of Santa Monica?"

"That I'm just following my beliefs?"

Niccole kicked Justyn again. "It's not funny. It wouldn't be good. They would use it against you."

"Then I won't get caught."

"You can be so cocky at times."

"I thought you liked those times?"

"JT."

"Ah. The food."

Dark Streets

Niccole and Justyn finished dinner an hour before the rendezvous with Jonas and Natalie and decided to use the time for Justyn to "score". Within twenty minutes of hitting the Promenade, Justyn had purchased a quarter bag - twenty dollars worth. He would get several joints with that amount. They came across Natalie and Jonas at a coffee shop that was featuring live music: one man and a keyboard. Natalie and Jonas had mistimed dinner also. The two couples listened to the music until the musician took a break.

After tipping the musician they strolled the Promenade, window shopping and talking. They forgo the ice cream and instead, returned to the coffee shop and live music. They had cake and coffee while the one man band created magic with synthesized sound.

When the musician went on his last break for the night, Justyn purchased two CD's, letting the musician keep the change out of a fifty dollar bill.

Justyn and Niccole couldn't stay for the last session, Rudy awaited them. Jonas and Natalie had declined the offer to smoke minutes earlier, they had other plans.

Justyn waved at Jonas, "See you in the morning, right?"

"Oh-nine-hundred," Jonas confirmed.

Niccole gave Natalie a quick hug and kiss.

"Enjoy the show," Niccole said.

"See you in the morning," Natalie nodded.

Outside the air had chilled, almost cool enough to see your breath. Justyn opened his sport jacket and pulled Niccole inside.

"This is cozy," she said.

"Wanna take the long way home?"

"Can't. Rudy."

"Duh."

"Did you smoke some of that already?"

"Funny."

They walked in silence as they turned the corner and headed up the short hill. Just across the next intersection a streetlight flickered off, then on, then off again, leaving a large section of the street dark.

Moments later, as they entered the dark circle, Justyn looked up and scanned the street ahead. Their building was at the end of the block. He could see the light on at Rudy's. He lowered his head to hear Niccole over the breeze.

"I'd really like to get a boat after all this," she said.

"That would be nice."

"I really liked the South Pacific. I don't know why."

"Probably because you can go topless all the time."

"Is not."

Unnatural silence surrounded them as they walked along the darkened street, a car idling a block up a side street the only sound other than their footfalls.

Justyn jerked when he heard a shotgun being pumped somewhere in front of them. Instinctively, he stepped in front of Niccole. He felt her bump into his back when he heard the gun blast. In the split-second between sound and impact, Justyn realized it had been aimed at him.

He felt heat more than force, but it was the force that shoved him back into Niccole. He heard her "Umphf". The heat spread through his body and he found he couldn't inhale. Nor exhale. Then they hit the ground. He could feel the blood flowing out of him. His life flowing out of him. He could feel Niccole beneath him. All the while, the heat inside him intensified.

She barely got an elbow down to break her fall, hearing it crack as it hit the concrete, an electric jolt shooting up her arm. Her head snapped back as the rest of her body hit. She heard her head crack, too, then everything went to a dim, dull fuzz. She heard a car drive up, men's voices, but couldn't discern what they were saying. Then the dimness expanded and she heard nothing but Justyn's gurgled breath. Moments later she heard footsteps running towards her. Then Justyn was being lifted off her. She heard him grunt and pulled him back to her.

"He's still alive, Miss Niccole." It was Rudy. "Let me

help."

She was still shaken, dazed from the impact, still trying to comprehend the situation. Her head and elbow hurt. She felt Justyn breathing on top of her, and his warm blood running down onto her. "No," Niccole said quietly, forcing it out. "He's fine. Get an ambulance. He's going to be fine."

"Okay, Miss Niccole," Rudy said, letting go of Justyn. "I have a waiter already call nine one one." He leaned over them, his hand on Justyn's wrist. "Did you see who did this to you?"

Niccole raised her head and put her lips next to Justyn's ear. "You hold on now, JT. You just lie there and let me hold you. You hold on. Help is on the way."

Justyn's breathing stopped. The blood quit spurting through Niccole's fingers. But more than that, she felt him go. She felt the life flow out him, as if his whole body sagged. At the same moment, in her head, although it felt like it was real, she was sailing with him, the sky and sea blue, blending into an indigo haze at the horizon. The spray soaking her chest.

She began to cry, squeezing Justyn's body close to her. Her throbs of anguish moved both of them. Rudy tried again to remove Justyn's body.

"NO!!!" Niccole screamed. She winced. Her head was pounding. Then softer, "Don't touch him. Leave him alone. Leave us alone." She started crying again, but more of a long, drawn sob. Tears streamed down her face, and her body jerked now and again, but else she was silent.

"Please, Miss Niccole, let me help you."

"Tell me you see him breathing, Rudy. Please, Rudy. Tell me you see him breathing. I'll believe you. Tell me.."

Tears choked off the rest.

Rudy placed his hand on hers. He looked at Justyn. The pellets hadn't separated very much. They reached from his chest to just above his belt, a few hitting his arms. He wasn't breathing. Rudy felt for a pulse. He tried a wrist, then the neck.

Reluctantly, slowly, Rudy said, "No pulse, Miss Niccole."

Her head was bleeding, badly. A small puddle was forming on the ground around the top of her head. She felt weak and suddenly very alone. She eased her grip on her dead husband.

"Let me help you. You are hurt, also." Rudy pulled Justyn's lifeless body off Niccole and laid him face down. Niccole moved to raise up, but grimaced in pain when she tightened her abdomen. A few of the pellets had gone through Justyn and into her. They weren't very deep, but deep enough to hurt. Her head was still throbbing and her elbow was sending long hot pins up her arm. She offered up her good arm to Rudy, "Please," she murmured.

Rudy gently helped Niccole stand, then aided her to the short wall along the sidewalk and helped her sit down on the pavement, her back against the wall. He went back to Justyn.

He turned him over onto his back, removed his host jacket and covered Justyn's torso. Niccole looked away.

Justyn's Wishes

"Leading our early AM newscast this morning is the
tragic death of gubernatorial candidate Justyn Thyme,
assassinated in Santa Monica near his home late last night.
Early reports say an anonymous caller tipped them off to a
white supremacy group. Authorities are saying all leads are
being checked out at this time. His wife, Niccole, escaped with
minor injuries."

*   *   *

In the early evening four days later, StoneAge Wizard

was heading for deep water. From her decks the sun was setting off starboard, between Santa Barbara and Santa Rosa Islands. The few clouds, high wisps of ice, were tinted hues of red, orange and pink.

The sails had been up for several hours, the California shoreline in a haze astern. Jonas was at the helm, Natalie and Niccole sat on the weather side in the cockpit. Justyn's body was lashed to the foredeck. They were headed to Amsterdam. Three days out they would give Justyn's body to the sea, then keep going.

*   *   *

"..When I die, Nicci, after many, many years of happiness with you, give my body to the salty brine and let me feed the fish one last time."

"That's gross, JT."

"Yeah. But that's what I want. I've lived off this planet my entire life, I owe it to her to give what little I have back."

- on the StoneAge Wizard, between Pitcairn and Los Angeles